THE MAIL-ORDER COWBOY'S SECOND CHANCE

IRON CREEK BRIDES

BOOK TWELVE

KARLA GRACEY

CONTENTS

This book is dedicated to all of my faithful readers, without whom I would be nothing. I thank you for the support, reviews, love, and friendship you have shown me as we have gone through this journey together. I am truly blessed to have such a wonderful readership.

CHARACTER LIST

- Elias Groves – tall
- Marta Pauling – slim
- Winton Groves – Elias' father
- Richard and Emily Ball – lawyer and wife
- Mary Ball – Richard's aunt
- Jonny and Cassie Cable – hotelier and wife
- Andrew and Amy Cable – newspaper owner and wife
- Mrs. Cable – the twins' mother
- Mayor Winston – Iron Creek's mayor
- Geoffrey and Jeannie Drayton – carpenter and wife
- Hank Wilson – postmaster
- Hector and Mary Jellicoe – townsfolk

- Thomas Jellicoe – postmaster's assistant
- Father Paul – priest
- Nelly Graham – town nurse and boarding house owner
- Garrett and Katy Harding – sheep farmers
- Zaaga – Garrett's Ojibwe adoptive mother
- Dibikad – Ojibwe friend of Garrett
- Alec Jenks – blacksmith
- Dr. Anna Jenks – town physician. Married to Alec Jenks
- Wesley and Clarice Baker – baker and wife
- Monsieur and Madame Lancelot – Wesley's mentor and wife
- Gertie Flitwick – assistant at the bakery
- Mr. Flitwick – reporter and Gertie's father
- Nelson and Bronwen Gustavson – bookstore owner and wife
- Warden Greenslade – prison warden
- Mr. Greenslade – ranch owner, brother of Warden Greenslade
- Hal – rancher for Mr. Greenslade
- Nev Hill – Elias' friend, a rancher
- Mr. Hill – Nev's father, ranch owner
- Millie – Nev's fiancée
- Frederick Lawson – Mr. Hill's lawyer
- Mrs. Rawlings – the Hills' housekeeper

- Enola – native American friend of Elias
- Mrs. Halfon – dressmaker
- Gerald Singer – station guard
- Dirk and Paul – Garrett Harding's shepherds

PROLOGUE

*J*anuary 17, 1872, Santa Fe, New Mexico

The courtroom was silent. Three men and a boy waited in the dock. The men were pale, their faces slick with fear induced sweat as they awaited their fate, yet young Elias could almost feel the eager anticipation of those in the gallery. He glanced up at his father beside him and wondered if his own face was as pale and drawn. Pop stared straight ahead. He'd not looked at Elias once since they'd been brought into the courtroom from their different jail cells. Elias wasn't sure if his father was mad at him, afraid for him, or actually ashamed that he had dragged such a young boy into this mess. He had never seen his brash, devil-may-care father look so afraid.

The gavel rapped sharply on the judge's desk in front of

them. Elias looked up at the man's stern face and began to shake when he saw him place a black cloth on his head.

"Winton Groves, Nile Highlander, and Walter Driscoll, for planning and implementing bank robbery, taking the money of hardworking, God-fearing people from the First National Bank of Santa Fe, I sentence you to hang by the neck, until you are dead, dead, dead."

The booming voice echoed around the room, followed by an excited whispering in the gallery. Elias looked up at his father. Tears were pouring down his cheeks as he looked down at Elias, took his hand, and squeezed it.

"I'm sorry, son," he whispered. "I'm so sorry."

The judge rapped his gavel three times and glared at everyone in the courtroom. "I have not finished." He gave a little cough to clear his throat, then looked directly at Elias, who felt the knots in his belly draw so tight he feared his stomach might rip into pieces. He, too, began to cry silent tears. "Elias Groves, ten-year-old boys have hung for less than the crimes that you have perpetrated. Yet I am inclined to show mercy. Your father has been very clear in his testimony, as have his accomplices, that you had no wish to be a part of their crimes." Pop squeezed Elias' hand more tightly. Elias could feel him shaking and couldn't help wondering which of them was more afraid. "Therefore, you will serve eight years in the Santa Fe jail. This is the verdict of the court." The judge brought his gavel down hard once more, then stood up and left the courtroom by a door behind his seat.

Pop sank to his knees. "Oh, Eli," he said, pulling Elias into his arms and hugging him close. "It's better than I could've ever hoped. I feared he would hang you along with the rest of us. We deserve it. You don't. You're just a boy, at the very start of your life, and I ruined that for you. I'm sorry."

"I know, Pop," Elias said. He buried his head in his father's shoulder and sobbed.

"Time to go," the sheriff said, pulling his father away.

"Give us one moment. I'm never going to see my boy again," Pop exploded, pulling away and hugging Elias even harder. Elias hugged him back. "Be good. When you get out, make a better life for yourself," Pop urged him. "Don't end up like me, swinging from a rope. You're better than that, better than me. Promise me, son?"

"I promise, Pop," Elias said.

The sheriffs took his father away, leaving Elias alone. Most of the people in the court were gone, too. He truly was all alone, and he felt very small and very frightened. A man in a prison uniform came into the dock. "Time to come with me," he said, his tone firm but with a hint of kindness. "You'll be in my care now. I'm Warden Greenslade."

Elias nodded and followed the man out through the back door of the courthouse, where a covered wagon was waiting.

The warden lifted Elias up into the back, then climbed in too. "Will my father be hanged soon?" Elias asked him.

"It won't be long, probably be on Friday. It'll be quick. He'll barely feel it." It was a kind lie, and Elias was grateful that the man had tried to soften things for him, but he'd seen men hang and knew how long they could be there struggling, their faces red and contorted with fear and pain, if the fall didn't break their necks. He hated to think of such an end for his father who, despite his inability to hold down a proper job and attraction to risk, had loved him. He had been a good father in every other way.

The warden reached into his pocket and pulled out a letter. "Can you read, lad?" he asked.

"Not really," Elias admitted, a little shamefacedly.

"Then I'll read this for you. When we get you settled, I'll teach you to read."

JANUARY 17, 1880, Santa Fe, New Mexico

Elias shivered as he stood in the yard, waiting for Warden Greenslade. The clothes that he had been given to leave in were thin, threadbare, and barely suitable for winter, but he had nothing else. The clothes he'd entered jail with hadn't fit him in years. Warden Greenslade emerged from the warmth of his office with a small suitcase in his hand, his ruddy cheeks pink, his hair graying just a little now.

"You have been a good lad, Groves. You've grown into a fine young man, and I've taught you all I can so that you can make an honest living out there," he nodded toward the door. "I hope never to see your face in a courtroom again."

"I'll do all I can," Elias assured him fervently. "Thank you for everything." And he meant it. Warden Greenslade and his men weren't used to having young boys around the place. Their charges came and went. Most went to the gallows. Nobody had stayed as long as Elias. Warden Greenslade had been like a stern, but friendly, uncle. "I'll write when I can."

"I'd like that," the warden said with a nod to the guard by the door. The man opened it. Warden Greenslade held out the suitcase to Elias.

"That's not mine," Elias said, giving the warden a quizzical look.

"It's just a few things to get you started out there, from myself and Mrs. Greenslade." Elias tried to protest, but the warden would not hear him. "Don't open it now. Do that once you get to the ranch. You remember the address?"

"I do," Elias said with a smile. "Thank you for finding me a place on your brother's ranch. You've already done more than enough for me, and now you do this, too." He shook his head as he took the suitcase from the warden.

"Good luck, Mr. Groves," the warden said with a smile. Elias was touched by that. He'd been Groves or Boy for so long. It felt nice to be shown a little respect. As he made his way out of the door, he vowed silently that he would do all he could to earn a little more of it.

He followed the directions Warden Greenslade had given him. It was a long walk, and the wind was bitter, slicing through the thin fabric of his pants and shirt. It took him almost two hours to reach the ranch, which looked vast and intimidating as he walked up the long driveway to the house. He knew his place, so he made his way around the back rather than stepping up onto the elegant wraparound porch at the front of the house. He was about to knock on the back door when a voice called out from behind him.

"You must be Jeb's boy."

Elias turned and saw a man who was the very spit and image of Warden Greenslade. "Yes, Sir," he said, reaching out a hand.

The man ignored it. "I'm not as soft-hearted as my brother. Heaven knows he should be a harder man, given his work," Mr. Greenslade said with a frown as he looked Elias over from top to toe. "You're a skinny little thing. Though I guess that's to be expected."

"Yes, Sir. I'm strong, though, Sir."

"You'll need to be. Ranching is hard work. Can you ride?"

"I can, Sir. Your brother taught me, and I can read and write."

"Only book a man needs to be able to read is the Bible, boy, and writing to sign his own name. No need for more,"

Mr. Greenslade said dismissively. Elias could hardly believe how different he was to his brother, even if they did look almost identical. "You'll attend church every Sunday, come rain or shine, sickness or health. I'll have no heathens on my property. And you'll be bunking in the barn."

He started to walk toward a large barn some way away from the house. Elias followed him. Mr. Greenslade opened a small door within the larger double doors and went inside, where he pointed to a ladder that led up to the hayloft. "You'll bunk up there. We start work at dawn."

With that, Elias was alone. He glanced around. There were cows in a couple of stalls – one had a calf with her – and there was hay piled almost everywhere. It was barely warmer than the courtyard outside, but he knew he wasn't in a position to complain. He had work and a place to stay, however terrible it might be. He climbed up the ladder and saw a bedroll laid out on the hay. Next to that was a box with an old skillet, a plate, and a knife and fork in it.

He sat down on the bed and wondered if he would ever get to live in a real house or sleep in a real bed. He'd spent eight years sleeping on a bedroll no better than this one. He'd hoped those days were behind him, but it seemed that even though Mr. Greenslade had seen it as his Christian duty to house and employ Elias, he did not believe that Elias deserved any more comfort than he'd had in jail. He knew that people wouldn't trust him until they knew him better, but he had hoped to be given the chance to win people over.

It seemed that was not going to be. How could he honor his promise to both his father and Warden Greenslade to make something of himself and to live an honorable and decent life if nobody could bring themselves to trust him?

He looked at the box of cooking utensils and wondered where he was supposed to actually use them? He couldn't set a fire in the barn, and he couldn't see a stove anywhere. Tired and hungry, he opened the suitcase and smiled when he saw a battered Stetson, a new pair of thick denim pants, and a flannel shirt. He lifted them out of the case and was surprised to see two new books, some paper, a pen, and some ink underneath. It was as if the warden had known all too well that his brother would not encourage such things in his ranch hand. It was a generous gift, and Elias was quick to dip the pen into the ink and write a letter of thanks to his dear mentor. He'd find a way to send it, somehow.

Just as he finished writing, he heard the clatter of the barn door opening and banging shut in the wind. "New boy," a deep, rather husky voice called. Elias peered over the edge. A man dressed in clothing somewhat similar to the things he had laid out on his bed was standing in the middle of the barn. "Get down here."

Elias did not hesitate to comply. He shinned down the ladder. "Yes, Sir," he said, as he stood in front of a stern and rugged looking man.

"I'm Hal," he said. "You're Elias?"

"I am."

"Well, Elias, I'll be teaching you everything you need to know."

"Thank you," Elias said.

"If you so much as set one foot out of line, you'll be out of here," Hal said gruffly. "Greenslade is a tough man, doesn't believe in being kind. He expects a lot. He pays badly. And he'll make sure you never get another job anywhere in New Mexico if you cross him."

"I'll not cross him."

"Best not to. Now, you'll be hungry, no doubt. There's a small outbuilding out back of this barn. In it, there's a small stove and a pantry with food. Us hands, we normally take turns cooking at night, but the rest of the day, you're on your own. No stealing another man's food." He gave Elias a look that said that everyone's eyes would be on him at all times – and even if it wasn't him that had taken something, because of his past, the blame would fall squarely upon his shoulders.

Elias frowned but said nothing. There was little point in saying anything. There was nowhere he could go that wouldn't treat him the same way. He would always be the boy who robbed a bank, even though all he'd done was act as a lookout because his father had insisted he do so. The few hopes he might have left jail with were dashed. This was his life now. One of suspicion and being the outsider. Nobody would ever trust him again. He was alone and would be alone for the rest of his days.

CHAPTER 1

pril 15, 1890, Iron Creek

Marta Pauling smiled as she watched her friend dancing with her new husband, surrounded by other loving couples and wondered if she would ever have a day like this one. It had been a wonderful wedding, and everyone was enjoying the party and the food, and she had received many compliments about the cake. It had been a labor of love for three entire days, but it had been worth it. She glanced over at the four layers of sponge with thick frosting and sugar roses. It was perfect, and both Emily and Richard had been delighted when they'd seen it.

She was so happy for them both and more than grateful that she had followed Emily to Iron Creek. Everyone was so friendly, and working with Wes in the bakery was a delight. He wanted to hear her ideas, and he had so much to teach her. The two of them were having so much fun that it was hardly like work at all. But with all the couples here in Iron Creek, she couldn't help feeling a little left out sometimes.

And it wasn't as if there were any eligible young men around who might want to marry her. They'd already found their loves, and at least half of them had done so via the matrimonial advertisements in the newspapers. She could hardly believe that such luck, so many happy endings, could occur in such a small town. Yet they had. The Cable twins and their wives, the Gustavsons, the Jenks, the Hansens, the Hardings, the Draytons, and even Wes and Clarice had all found one another because of advertisements. It was a little too much luck for such a small town, perhaps, but Marta couldn't help hoping that there was perhaps enough of whatever magic had brought them all together was still strong, so that she, too, might find love. If only she could bring herself to post the advertisement that she'd spent weeks composing.

Emily sank down into a chair beside her, breathing heavily. "That man can really dance," she said happily.

"So, you're enjoying being Mrs. Ball?" Marta teased.

"So far," Emily said with a grin. "Have you seen my father and Mrs. Ball? He's being very attentive."

Marta glanced over to where Mayor Winston, Emily's father, was sitting with Richard's aunt. The older woman looked very well considering she'd suffered from apoplexy just a few months earlier. The two were laughing and having a wonderful time. "They make a sweet couple."

"Yes, they do," Emily said. "I'm trying to decide if I think it would be a wonderful thing if they were to fall in love."

"I think it would be," Marta said firmly. "Your father deserves to be happy, and Mrs. Ball is kind and generous and very pretty, for an older lady."

"It must have been so hard for him and my mother, thinking that the other was dead. I still find it hard to believe that my father never remarried."

"He was heartbroken, but it seems that having you back in his life has mended some of that pain."

"Then we will wish them both well and hope that they do, indeed, fall head over heels in love," Emily decided. "And we need to find you a husband, too."

"No, we do not," Marta said firmly. She was not sure that she wanted anyone to know that she was considering doing just that.

"You are the most romantic person I know," Emily said, her eyes wide with surprise. "Don't you want to be happy? To be loved, as Richard loves me?"

"Of course I do," Marta said. "But I am not ready for it yet. Give me time to settle. I'm enjoying my work and being here. For the moment, that is enough."

"If you say so," Emily said with a grin. "I don't believe you, but I'll not do anything on your behalf. Poor Richard was so mortified when he found out what his uncle had done, placing an advertisement on Richard's behalf, even though it all turned out so beautifully for us. So you don't need to fear that."

"I am glad."

"Now, come and dance with Richard. I want to dance with my father," Emily said, getting up and holding out her hand. Marta took it and let Emily pull her to her feet and drag her across the room to where Richard was talking to Jonny Cable.

"Marta wants to dance," Emily said to her husband. "You don't mind, do you?"

"Not at all," Richard said with a warm smile. Marta glared a little at Emily, who just giggled and went to fetch her father.

Richard really was an excellent dancer, and it made Marta think that perhaps it was a skill that she might like her future husband to have. It wasn't something she'd particularly considered before, but it felt magical to be whirled around the room with such grace. When the music stopped, she was breathless and a little more envious of Emily than before. Richard was such a good man – kind, clever, and a real gentleman.

"Thank you," he said, bowing to her as she gave him a bobbed curtsey. "And thank you for the cake and all the food. You and Wes have truly given us a banquet worthy of kings."

"No, just worthy of my best friend and the best man I know," Marta said, and gave him a kiss on the cheek.

"Thank you for making Em so happy."

"She makes me happy," he said softly. "I didn't know I needed anyone, but my uncle was right after all. I should have listened. It was a rare day when he wasn't." He looked sad for a moment.

"I am sure he knows that it all worked out for the best."

"Aunt Mary often says that, too," Richard said. "We both miss him very much, especially today. I am sure he would have loved Emily. She's very like my aunt in a lot of ways."

Just then, Nelly Graham whisked him away so that he and Emily could cut the cake. Marta tried not to wince as the knife sliced through her masterpiece, but she enjoyed watching everyone eat their slices with evident pleasure. Being a baker was a peculiar calling. You created beautiful things, then had to watch them being destroyed with such delight. It was bittersweet that nothing she made ever lasted long and all she had were memories of her work.

Not long after, it was time for everyone to go home. Marta kissed Emily and Richard goodbye and began to walk down the road to the village. Andy Cable and his wife stopped and offered her a ride, which she gladly accepted.

"It was a lovely wedding," Amy said with a sigh.

"What was yours like?"

"A little hurried," Amy said with a fond smile at her husband.

"We can arrange something to celebrate it in more style

if you wish?" Andy said. "I don't want you to feel that you missed out on anything."

"I didn't. I love big weddings, but ours was perfect," Amy said. "Not everyone needs the entire town to be there and a big, beautiful cake. However did you make it so tall without it collapsing?"

"Ah, I cannot give away the secrets of our trade or everyone will be able to make their own cakes," Marta joked.

"Keep your secrets, then," Amy said with a grin. "I don't think any of us could make things taste as delicious as you and Wes do, even if we knew how. The two of you are very clever."

"Thank you," Marta said, feeling a little embarrassed by all the praise. "I do love what I do."

They dropped her off at the mayor's house, which was still dark. Clearly, Mayor Winston had not yet returned. Marta let herself in and lit the lamps in the hallway and up the stairs. She went straight up to bed. It had been a wonderful day, but the stress of getting everything right for Emily had taken its toll. She was tired and longed for her bed.

She undressed quickly, dropping her gown and petticoats on the floor where they fell, then sank into her bed. As she reached out to turn out the lamp, she saw the notepad in which she'd been trying to write her advertisement on the table beside her. She picked it up and looked at the one that she'd decided was the best of the hundred she'd written over the past weeks and added a few words about enjoying dancing. She read it out loud a couple of times to hear how it sounded. She did not want to sound too desperate or as if she was better than she was. But was she brave enough to send it?

She put it down on the table and turned out the lamp. In the darkness, she looked up at the ceiling for a few moments. It was strange how important finding a husband had become to her. She'd never much thought about it until Emily and Richard had fallen in love. She'd been content with her life as it was. Despite that, she had read all the romance stories in the newspapers and even bought cheap romance books at the local booksellers, dreaming that one day she would find her one true love. That was all it had been, though, a distant dream, a hope for the future. But now, she could see everything that she was missing out on. Yet still, she hesitated.

She had been thinking about why she'd not chosen to follow the path of becoming a mail-order bride all those years ago when her uncle had wanted her to marry Jake. He had been only a year or two younger than her uncle, fat, drank too much, and beaten the animals on the farm. She had not wanted to marry him and had longed to find a way to escape. She hadn't placed an advertisement, or responded to one, for fear that if she took such a chance, there might be someone even worse at the other end of the letters, no matter how wonderful he seemed on paper. And that fear was still there, even with all the positive stories that Iron Creek provided about how wonderfully well things could work out.

Marta closed her eyes and took a couple of long, deep breaths. She would worry about it all in the morning. Tonight, she just wanted to sleep. She turned onto her side and curled up under the blankets. She reached out a hand and stroked the sheets beside her, wondering what it would be like to have someone there who loved her, whom she loved in return. But to make that happen, she needed to be courageous, and she wasn't sure if she could be. It was such a big step. Such an important thing. And would any man accept a woman who loved her career as much as she did? Would they be happy to always come second to the bakery and its demands?

She rolled over onto her other side and pulled a pillow over her head, wishing the thoughts would just stop. But it seemed that she was not to be blessed with sleep. Her mind raced, thinking of all that could go wrong. She had to force herself to remember how wonderful it could be if it went right. She thought about everyone she'd met in Iron Creek and how happy they were because they had taken a risk to find someone who could make them whole. And every single one of them would tell her to take the chance for love. She knew that.

Marta knew that her new friends would do all they could to keep her safe if things did not work out. She had been alone before, when she had been barely more than a girl. She should have been able to rely upon her uncle to do what was best for her, not for himself and his drunk friend. He had forced her to take charge of her own life, and she had done so very well, even though doing it all alone had been hard. But she was no longer alone. She had friends now, people who would fight for her if she needed them to. If she did not try, she would never know if it could work out or not.

Exhaling sharply, she sat up and thrust the pillow to one side. She fumbled a little in the dark to light the lamp again, then got up and pulled out her writing desk from under the bed. She pulled out a sheet of paper and began to write a letter, copying the wording of her advertisement in her notebook. When she had finished, she folded and sealed it and put it on the bedside table before putting her desk back below the bed.

"I'll take you to the newspaper tomorrow," she said to the letter. "Now, let me sleep."

CHAPTER 2

April 24, 1890, Lake Nighthorse, Colorado

The herd were grazing down by the lake. "Am I glad this day is done and that we're nearly home," Nev said as he and Elias dismounted not far away. Elias bent down and splashed his face with the cold water. It made him gasp, but it was refreshing after a long day in the saddle. "I'll get some kindling for a fire while you keep watch. There's Indians nearby."

Elias nodded, and the rangy cowboy went in search of some dry wood to make a fire on the shore. Elias had driven cattle through these parts a few times before. He knew that there were Navajo and Ute tribes nearby. In fact, the first time he'd driven cattle through these lands, he'd found a young Indian girl with a broken leg not far from Lake

Nighthorse. She'd been so afraid of him and Wally, the man he'd been driving the herd with that time, but Elias had done what he could to soothe her and taken her back to her people. They'd been cautious, but grateful, and now they let him be.

As he untied the bedrolls from behind his and Nev's saddles, he saw a young woman a little way along the shore. She had long, dark hair and wore a brightly colored shawl around her shoulders. Elias recognized her immediately. It was Enola, the girl he'd helped all those years ago. When he walked to meet her, she smiled shyly at him.

"I didn't know if it would be you with the herd," she said. "I come every time I see the cattle here at the lake. It isn't always you."

"No," Elias said with a smile. "I don't always work here. I move all around New Mexico, Colorado, Utah, and Arizona."

"I'm glad to see you."

"And I, you," he said. "You look well."

She grinned at him and opened her shawl slightly so he could see her rounded belly. "I'm going to name him for you if it is a boy."

"Well, I am mighty flattered," he said, shaking his head in surprise. The last time he'd seen Enola, she had been trying to choose between two of the young men of her tribe who both wanted her hand. "That is wonderful for you. You made your choice, then?"

"I am with Mato," she said happily.

"Mato?" he asked. He didn't remember him being one of the two men.

"The son of Dasan," she said. "He will be chief like his father one day."

"He is a good man?"

"He is. A very good man."

"I am happy for you, Enola," Elias said warmly. "But you'd best go before my companion comes back. He does not hold any love for your people. His brother was killed by an Apache, and he holds a grudge against all the native tribes now."

"I'll go. I am glad I got to see you, and to tell you my news."

Elias watched her walk away. Enola had become a lovely young woman, and he would always care for her. And his connection with the local tribe made bringing herds through this area much safer and easier, though he rarely explained to his companions why. Too many cowboys were afraid of the tribes, some with justification, but mostly because of ignorance. And the tribes were understandably unhappy that the White men were taking over their ancestral lands and forcing them onto reservations. Elias was glad that, at least here, he did not need to worry about those tensions becoming too great. He was sure that there had to be a better way for both sides to live together, but his voice counted for nothing. He was no more than an itinerant cowboy, after all.

Nev returned with an armful of kindling and dry wood and began to build a fire on the shore. "It's nice here," he said as he blew gently on the kindling to get it to catch. A few flames flickered, so he began carefully adding more kindling and wood. Elias handed him a kettle and some tin mugs from their saddlebags, then rummaged deeper to find the coffee and sugar.

Nev filled the kettle with water from the lake and placed it in the fire to boil while Elias set a line to catch fish from the lake for their breakfast in the morning. The easiest thing to hunt here were rabbits, so he went in search of their supper. He soon had four, which he took back to the shore, where he skinned and gutted them deftly. Nev took them from him and cut them up into pieces, then added them to a pot he'd hung over the fire from a tripod.

"Last of the onions and carrots," he said sadly. "But hopefully, we'll be back at the ranch by tomorrow night."

"It's been a good drive," Elias said. He sat down on his bedroll by the fire and took a mug of coffee from Nev.

"Will you be sticking around?"

"I don't know," Elias said. "I'm hoping Mr. Hill will want me to. I like this part of the world."

"I'll definitely put in a good word for you with Dad," Nev assured him. "I've not worked with a better cowboy."

"Thank you," Elias said, though he wasn't sure that his skills would ever be enough for some ranch owners. Once they found out about his past, he was out of work again.

That was why he traveled around now, just helping out on drives, never really staying in one place too long. He'd tried to make a home for himself and been driven out of them too many times to get attached to any place now.

"Where'll you go if he doesn't keep you on?"

"I don't know. There are a couple of ranches up in Utah that do drives this time of year. I'd maybe go there. And there are always farms that want laborers at this time of year."

They fell into a companionable silence as they waited for their food to cook. Occasionally, Elias got up to check the fishing line. By the time the rabbit was tender, they had four plump fish gutted and cooking on a thin, flat stone in the fire so they would be ready for their breakfast the next day. Nev served them each a bowl of rabbit stew, and they ate it hungrily.

"Will Millie be there to meet you tomorrow?" Elias asked.

"I hope so. It's been too long to be away from her," Nev said with a rather goofy smile as he thought about his fiancée. "I'll be glad when I don't have to drive cattle across the state line every few months."

"Your father said he'd pass the running of the ranch over to you once you're married, didn't he?"

"He did, though I doubt he'll be able to keep his nose out of things for too long. I'll just be glad to be able to sleep in my own bed, with my wife beside me, every night of the year."

"I don't think that's in my future," Elias said, trying to make his tone light. "I envy you."

"Find yourself a rancher's daughter and marry her, then you can do the same," Nev joked.

"I doubt there's many men who'd let me within a hundred miles of their daughters." Elias couldn't help feeling a little bitter that he was still being punished for a crime he'd been given no choice but to take part in as a boy. He'd been given a start at the Greenslade Ranch, and he'd learned his trade and done all he was told, but Warden Greenslade had passed away unexpectedly and within a day of his old mentor's funeral, Mr. Greenslade had thrown Elias off his property. Despite being good at his job, nobody wanted him on their ranch after that, and though he'd been able to find work on cattle drives from time to time, he knew he would never be made a permanent hand anywhere.

"You're a good man," Nev said firmly. "I know your name isn't held in much esteem, and Dad was wary about taking you on because of it, but in my eyes you've more than made up for what your father made you do. Once I'm in charge, you've a place with us as long as you live."

"Thank you," Elias said. He and Nev had talked a lot, usually over too much whiskey, about the troubles he'd faced in his life. Nev was a good man, despite his fear and hatred of the tribes, and a good listener. Elias had rarely had anyone he could call a friend in his life, but Nev had definitely become one. "I'll not hold you to that, though."

"You can hold me to it, but why don't you think about getting away from here altogether? Start somewhere new, where they don't know your name before you even walk through the door? I'll gladly give you a letter of recommendation to take with you."

"I've thought about it, but I wonder how far I'd need to go to outrun my name."

"Montana? Washington? Maine?" Nev said with a grin. "Maybe even get a new name."

"No, I like my name," Elias said. "A man needs to accept every part of himself, including his past."

"That's all well and good, as long as others do the same," Nev said pointedly. "You're not the actions of a ten-year-old boy doing his father's bidding. You're a grown man. You work hard, you are good and decent, and you deserve better."

Elias gave his friend a weak smile. "Maybe you're right. Perhaps I should find a wife with a good dowry to bring me," he joked.

"There's bound to be someone out there who'll accept you as you are. If I can find a woman who loves me despite my gangly limbs and skinny face, you'll have no trouble with that handsome face of yours."

"It helps that your father owns the biggest ranch in New

Mexico," Elias said with a laugh. "I see your point, but where does a man like me find a wife?"

"In the newspaper," Nev said solemnly. "There's men all over the country that place advertisements for a bride. Why not you?"

"Why not me?" Elias echoed. "And, as you say, the further away she is, the less chance there is of my past catching up to me. I could start again. Get a second chance. But it's crazy to have to go to such lengths."

"It is, but you're not really in a position to think about anything else. Besides, you can always come and work for me if it doesn't work out."

Nev lay down, pulled his blanket over his body, and was snoring loudly within moments. Elias sat up for a while, gazing into the glowing embers of the fire as he thought about all they had talked about. It was definitely something worth considering, going further north where he might be able to get a new start. Though he'd accepted long ago that he would never marry, he might have a chance at finding love if he was able to keep his past a secret.

He wasn't sure that he dared to hope that such a thing could happen to him. He had spent too many years of his life accepting the scraps that others were willing to throw his way to think he might deserve more. He tried to be good, to honor his father's final wishes, and to honor Warden Greenslade, who had done all he could to try to give him a new start in life. He worked hard when he could get work.

He was polite and helped out anyone he could. Yet as soon as anyone knew that he'd been in jail, all they saw was a criminal, and rarely did anyone let him explain. Nev was one of the few men who'd ever cared to hear about all that had really happened, all those years ago. He hadn't turned away. But Nev was unusual in many ways.

Unable to sleep, he lit a torch from the fire and went to check on the cattle. They were content enough, munching on grass or lying down on the soft grass by the lake. He did a quick head count. Two were missing – one of the cows and her calf. With a heavy sigh, he began to look for them. He walked for miles around the lake until he reached the Navajo camp. There were still a few fires glowing and people milling around. At first, they glared at him and began to move toward him, appearing intent on driving him away. When he gave them a friendly wave, one of the men recognized him and waved back.

"Have you seen a cow and her calf?" he called out to them.

They shook their heads. "Try over the hill. There's a small crevasse, they may be stuck there," one of them called back.

"Thank you," Elias called back, already heading in the direction he'd pointed.

He climbed up the hill, away from the lake, and soon found the crevasse, but there was no sign of the animals. He walked along the ridge of the hill, looking down and around him until he saw a small outcrop of rocks near a thicket. The dense trees and bushes were just the place that a curious calf might get caught in. As he drew nearer, he heard an anguished mooing. He hurried toward the desperate cries, pulling out the knife from his belt to cut through some of the dense branches. The cow and her calf were huddled together by some rocks.

"Well, there you are," he said to them with a sigh of relief. He glanced around and saw some of the undergrowth had been trampled. Clearly, that was the way they had come in, but why they hadn't found their way back out was unclear.

The cow stood up and nudged the calf. The little one did not move and just mewled at his mother. Elias knelt down beside the calf. "What's up with you, little one?" he asked. He began to feel down the animal's spine and legs. The calf cried out as he ran his hand down the back right leg, and the cow nudged Elias away from her baby. "It's alright, Mama," he said to her in a gentle voice. "We're going to help him. If you'll just let me."

He didn't know if she understood him or not, but she let him pick the calf up and followed him back to the camp. Elias splinted the calf's leg and kept the two of them close, away from the rest of the cattle. An injured calf could all too easily get trampled by the rest.

"You rest here tonight, and we'll be back at the ranch tomorrow," he said to them. He brought his bedroll over to sleep by them. "Just you stay still for me. You need to rest that leg. If your mama will let me, I'll take you up on Jet tomorrow so you don't have to walk." He reached out and stroked both animals gently until all three of them were asleep.

CHAPTER 3

*A*pril 25, 1890, Lake Nighthorse, New Mexico

The two men were up with the dawn. Elias checked the calf's leg while Nev packed up the saddlebags and bedrolls, then they sat down to eat the fish they'd cooked the night before. Elias took the calf with him on Jet. The horse was strong and hardy and didn't complain about the extra weight. Slowly, the men circled the herd and began to drive them south toward the New Mexico border. The days were long when on a cattle drive, but both men hoped to cover the final twenty-three miles in one day. They longed for a comfortable bed and home-cooked meal. To cover that far in a day would mean that nothing could go wrong, but at least the cattle did not need to reach the ranch rested, as would be the case if they were going the other way. They could rest once they got to the ranch.

They covered the distance with relatively few incidents considering the pace they were moving at. From time to time, a couple of the calves got left behind or went off exploring, but they were soon retrieved. By the time the sun was beginning to go down, they could see the ranch in the distance. They covered the last few miles with light hearts, knowing that they could soon rest. Mr. Hill was waiting at the gate to the pen. Nev and Elias herded the cattle into it, and the older man shut the gate behind them.

When the mother of the calf in Elias' lap came to the gate, Elias moved Jet closer to the cow so she could see her baby.

"What's this?" Mr. Hill asked him.

"Little one went exploring, and his mama followed him into a thicket last night. He must have fallen on the rocks. I splinted the leg and brought them both back to the herd. It might be an idea to put them in a stall tonight," Elias said.

Mr. Hill nodded a little grudgingly. Nev dismounted and slipped a halter over the cow's head before his father opened the gate and let her out. Mr. Hill held his arms up for the calf. Elias handed him down, then dismounted and took the calf back from him.

"Come on up to the house for supper tonight, Elias," Mr. Hill said, turning his back and walking back to the sprawling ranch house. "Mrs. Hill has made chicken pot pie."

"Thank you, Sir," Elias said, surprised at such an invitation. Mr. Hill had never invited him to the house before, even though Elias had driven cattle across state lines for him, to the markets in Colorado, Kansas, Texas, and Oklahoma more than a dozen times.

"You've impressed him," Nev said once they had taken the cow and her calf to the barn and settled them in a pen, then rubbed down their horses and put them in stalls with plenty of food. "He cares for his animals, and you've shown him you do, too."

"You'd think he knows that, given how many times I've driven his herds," Elias said with a wry smile. "Why else would he trust me with them?"

"He didn't, until today," Nev said with a grin. "He trusted me, and he knows I like doing the drive with you. You never know, he may even find you a permanent place now – or at least, he won't complain too much when I give you one."

"I can only hope," Elias said. "It would be nice to stay in one place for a while. It's been a long time since I could say that anywhere was home."

Nev went inside the house, and Elias made his way to the bunkhouse. He lit a fire in the grate, brought in the old tin bath from outside and put it in front of the fire. He fetched some water from the well in the yard and poured it into the tub and put a couple of pails over the fire to boil. He sank down on his bed as he waited, suddenly feeling every ache in his body from the weeks of sleeping rough and being on horseback. He stripped off his clothes, poured the boiling water into the bath, along with a bucket of cold, and sank into the warm water; his legs hanging over the sides of the small, narrow tub.

He lathered up some soap and washed every inch of his body and his hair, then used a jug to pour water over his head to rinse off the suds. Once he had dried himself in front of the fire and gotten dressed in some clean pants, he dragged the tub out of the bunkhouse and emptied it on the ground, then used some fresh hot water to shave. Feeling a lot better, he pulled on his best shirt and made his way over to the house.

He knocked on the door, and Mr. Hill opened it a few moments later. "It's good to see that you scrub up well," he said with a grin. "I'm not sure I've ever seen you clean-shaven and bathed from head to toe."

"It's a little hard to do on a drive," Elias said.

"And you don't often stay around afterward, like some of the other cowboys do."

"No, I go where the work is," Elias said.

"Well, Neville tells me he'd like you to stick around this time. Do you think you could do that?"

"I'd like to, Sir."

"I know about your past," Mr. Hill said, his expression suddenly serious. "I know that you've struggled to escape it, and I'll not say that it makes me happy. But Neville is sure that you are the kind of man he wants here when he takes over the running of this place, and I trust his judgment, but

I'd rather see how you go before I hand over everything to him."

"I understand, Sir," Elias said. "I'd want to be sure I'm trustworthy and hardworking, too."

"Even a hint that you're not the law-abiding man you claim to be, and you'll be out," Mr. Hill warned him. "I'll not tolerate thieving."

"I've never stolen anything," Elias said firmly. "If Neville told you of my past, you know that. I was to keep watch only, and I could not gainsay my father, as Neville would never gainsay you."

Mr. Hill nodded, then showed Elias through to a large dining room, where he poured an inch of whiskey into three glasses. He handed one to Elias and took one himself. He took a sip. Elias did the same. The whiskey was smooth and rich, with a smoky, earthy flavor. It was the best whiskey Elias had ever drunk. He took another sip.

"Nothing like the hooch you boys take on the drive," Mr. Hill said with a smile. "I remember that stuff all too well. It could strip the rust off iron and made your mind forget all the hardships of the day, but it kept you warm inside on a cold night."

"It does do that," Elias agreed as Nev entered the room with a pretty brunette on his arm.

"Good evening," Nev said to them both. He took the third glass of whiskey and drank it in one gulp. "Elias, this is my Millie."

Millie smiled at Elias, and Elias gave her a nodding bow. "It is a pleasure. Neville has talked of you often. He missed you very much."

"I am glad to hear it, but I am even happier that I will never have to say goodbye to him for so long ever again," Millie said. "I worry so when he is gone."

"I take good care of him," Elias assured her. "And he's a surprisingly good cook."

They all laughed. Mrs. Hill joined them and indicated that they should take their seats. A young woman, no more than nineteen, appeared with a large tureen of soup. She placed it on the sideboard, then took a bowl at a time from the table and filled it with thick, potato, and leek soup. Elias watched for a moment, waiting to see if the Hills said grace. Mrs. Hill closed her eyes and clasped her hands in front of her. Mr. Hill did the same, followed by Millie. Nev grinned at Elias, and the two of them followed suit.

"Dear Lord and Father, thank you for the blessings you have brought to this family. We are grateful for the food in front of us and the company we keep. Keep us safe. Amen," Mrs. Hill said reverently.

"Amen," everyone echoed softly.

"Now, eat," she said with a warm smile. Nev picked up his spoon and began scooping the soup into his mouth quickly, as if he'd not eaten in a month. Millie ate more daintily, as did Mrs. Hill. Mr. Hill ate almost as heartily as his son, but Elias knew that it did not mean that he could. He ate carefully, as Warden Greenslade and his wife had taught him to do all those years ago. He dipped his spoon at the edge of the bowl and sipped at the soup rather than slurping it as he longed to do. It was delicious, warm, and comforting. Just the kind of food a man craved when away from home for a long time.

As promised, the main course was chicken pot pie, Nev's favorite. The pastry was rich with butter, crisp, and melted in the mouth, the chicken was succulent, and the thick sauce was rich and satisfying. Elias could honestly say that he had never eaten food so delicious in his life. His eyes almost popped out of their sockets when the dessert was brought in – a delicate confection of sponge and cream with sugared roses and marzipan. He could hardly believe such a thing could be real. And it was like eating a slice of heaven on earth.

When the dishes had been cleared away, the two women left the men in the dining room. Mr. Hill took a silver cigar box from inside the sideboard and offered it to Elias and Nev.

"You have much better table manners than I was expecting," Mr. Hill said as he lit Elias' cigar.

"I was taught by a fine man, many years ago," Elias said.

"He did a good job," Mr. Hill said. "A much better one than it seems I have managed with Neville," he added drily as he lit his son's cigar, too.

"I can behave when I have to," Nev grumbled. "But I

shouldn't have to when I come back to my own home after months away."

"It amazes me why Millie wants to marry you," Mr. Hill teased his son.

"When is the wedding?" Elias asked.

"Next week," Nev said with a mock look of fear. "You'll come, of course?"

"I wouldn't miss it," Elias said with a smile as Mr. Hill handed them both a glass of brandy.

They drank and smoked in silence, savoring the pleasures of both for a few minutes, but Nev suddenly jumped up from his seat. "Dad, where is today's newspaper?" he asked excitedly. "We need to find Elias a wife, too."

"No, we do not," Elias said firmly. "Your father has offered me a job, so I've no need to find a wife right now."

"Nonsense," Mr. Hill said. "Every man needs a good woman. Even if you stay here, you'll want a wife one day. It takes time to find the right one, so you'd best start looking now." He looked over to his son. "The newspaper is in my study, on my desk."

Nev fetched it and spread it open on the mahogany table. "Hmm," he said, running a finger down the page of matrimonial advertisements. "How about this one? Young lady seeks gentleman for marriage, must have excellent prospects and a full head of hair." He laughed and glanced at Elias. "Well, I suppose you do have a fine head of hair."

"Any young woman with even half an ounce of sense

would not consider a man like me," Elias said. "I've nothing to offer anyone."

"But you could have," Mr. Hill said softly. "When I met my wife, I had barely a nickel to my name. All I had was dreams. With her by my side, I had a reason to reach for more."

"I can reach all I like, but it's not going to make men trust me once they know I was in jail for eight years," Elias said bitterly. "What woman could possibly want a man like me?"

"You need to stop thinking that way," Nev said. "We trust you. We're glad to know you, and we know about your past."

"Your father doesn't trust me, not fully," Elias said.

"No, I don't," Mr. Hill said. "But I don't trust Neville fully either. A man is a fool if he blindly trusts anyone other than himself. But I have faith in you. I believe that you mean what you say when you tell us that you want a better life. All you need to do is to find a woman who can say the same. Take the newspaper to the bunkhouse with you. Perhaps you'll find someone to write to without us breathing down your neck."

CHAPTER 4

May 14, 1890, Iron Creek, Minnesota

It had been a busy day in the bakery. Wednesday was market day in Iron Creek, which meant that the town was full of people. They came by carriage, wagon, and train, and every one of them wanted to fill their baskets with treats from the bakery. Marta sank into a chair by the fire and closed her eyes for a moment. Mayor Winston came out of his study across the hall and peered around the door of the parlor. "Would you like a cup of tea?" he asked her kindly.

"Oh, that would be heaven," she said. "With a slice of the cake I left on the kitchen table, perhaps?"

"Is it the cherry one again? I do so love that one."

"No, it is a new recipe we've been working on, apple and spice," she said. "I think you'll like it."

"It sounds delicious," Mayor Winston said, licking his lips. "I am so very glad you decided to stay here with me once Emily got married."

"I'm glad you wanted me to," Marta said. She meant it. It had been very kind of him to offer her a home even though his daughter had moved into her husband's newly renovated house on the edge of town.

"I like having company," he said. "It is so lovely to know there is someone else in the house."

"Even if I am rarely awake at normal hours?" she said with a grin.

"Even though you wake me up in the middle of the night when you go to work," he joked back before heading to the kitchen.

Marta stood up and stretched her body. Everything ached, and she wondered if she would feel better after a hot bath in front of the fire in her room, but her thoughts were interrupted by a knock on the front door. When she went out into the hallway and opened the door, Hank Wilson, the town's postmaster, was standing on the porch.

"Good afternoon, Miss Pauling. I do hope you are well."

"I am, thank you, Mr. Wilson," she said.

"I have some letters for you and a parcel for Mayor Winston," he said, reaching into the battered leather satchel he wore across his chest. He pulled out a neatly tied package and three letters and handed them to her. "Will you both be at the theater tomorrow night?"

"I believe we will be," Marta said. "It is rather wonderful having our very own theater company, isn't it?"

"It is. Though, I sometimes think the town has changed beyond all recognition. So many people here now, so much going on. It's hard for an old man to keep up." He gave a wan smile.

"You should hire an assistant," Marta said to him. "Perhaps Thomas Jellicoe? He'd be able to do your deliveries for you, he's got plenty of energy."

"That is actually a very good idea, Miss Pauling. I might just do that." He tipped his hat and went on his way.

Marta went into the kitchen. Mayor Winston was just pouring boiling water into the teapot. She put the parcel at the head of the table and her letters down by her usual chair, then fetched a knife from the drawer and plates from the larder and cut two generous slices from the apple cake and put one in front of each chair. She sat down and opened the first of her letters. It was from a farmer in Idaho who wanted a good and docile wife to raise his twin sons and cook and clean for him. She immediately put it to one side. She had nothing against the idea of marrying a man who already had children, but she was most certainly not a homely, biddable wife, and nor did she ever wish to be such a thing.

"What have you got there?" Mayor Winston said. He poured out the tea and pushed a cup across the table to her before sitting down.

"Just some letters," she said. "I put an advertisement in

the newspaper. To be honest, I didn't really expect anyone to write back, but it seems that there are three men in the world who think I might be interesting enough to write to."

"You're hoping to marry, too?" he said, looking a little sad at the thought. "But then you'll leave me as well, and I've only just got used to having my girls around me."

Marta was flattered that he thought of her as a daughter of sorts. She'd barely known her own father, and the portly mayor was kind and generous, the kind of man she'd often imagined her father to be. "I've no intention of leaving any time soon," she said, reaching out her hand and giving his a reassuring squeeze. "You're stuck with me until you get the courage to ask Mrs. Ball to be your wife."

"I don't know what you mean," he said, looking pink and flustered. "I've never suggested that anything of the sort might occur."

"No, you haven't, but you cannot deny that you like her, and she likes you. Em and me, well, we saw you together at the wedding and thought you'd make a lovely couple."

"Nonsense," Mayor Winston blustered. "She is a fine lady and we get on well, but there really is nothing more to it than that."

Marta tried to stifle a giggle by stuffing a large chunk of cake into her mouth. "Well, whatever you say," she said when she'd finished it. She handed him the letter she'd already discarded. "I don't think he'll suit me, do you?"

While he read the first letter, she opened the second one.

This man seemed much more interesting. He was not sure he was ready for marriage but would very much like to share a correspondence so they might get to know one another better. His lack of haste appealed to her, and the fact that he was a cowboy intrigued her. So many of the heroes in the romance stories she loved so much were cowboys, all rugged and manly yet sensitive and kind. She wanted to know if such men really did exist in real life. The third sounded duller than the first, so she was able to discard him with no qualms. But what could she possibly write in a letter to a complete stranger?

"None of them sound good enough for you," Mayor Winston declared once he'd read them all. "But if you must write to anyone, this one is probably the best of the three." He held up the third letter. "He works in accounts, so he is probably diligent and good with money."

"The man so dull I almost fell asleep reading his letter?" she asked.

"He sounds reliable."

"I am not looking for reliability as a man's primary trait," Marta said. "Staid has its place in life, but it doesn't do much to rouse the heart."

"I suppose you are right, but this cowboy, well, they're not known for being that reliable," he said anxiously. "Though, I'm guessing his letter is the one you most want to reply to."

"I do. He sounds interesting. He will have some stories,

at least, and not just tell me of financial balances he's totted up. I promise I will not marry any man who you do not deem worthy of me." She grinned at him, and he grinned back.

"You joke of such things, but I worry about you. I am so lucky that Emily chose such a fine man. I did not need to worry about her happiness for even a moment."

"And you need not worry about mine. This is just a little fun. If anything comes of it, I shall be sure to ask you to interrogate him fully before I make any final decision."

"You will do what you want, whatever I say," he grumbled. "But you are a sensible girl, for all your romantic notions. I'm sure you'll not do anything silly."

"I am glad to have your blessing for my romantic notions. Now, go and call on Mrs. Ball and ask her if she would like to see the ducks on the creek."

"I'm not sure her wheeled chair would make it as far as the creek," Mayor Winston said thoughtfully.

"It may not, but she is walking quite well now, Emily told me this morning. She and Richard do not always have enough time in the daylight hours to walk with her, though."

The seed sown, Marta kissed him on the cheek and went upstairs to get ready for bed. For many, it was only late afternoon, but for her, it was almost bedtime. She would be up before dawn to fire up the ovens and start the day's preparations in the bakery. And she had a letter to write before she curled up and closed her eyes.

She undressed quickly and smiled when she heard the

click of the front door as Mayor Winston let himself out of the house. She hoped he was going to see Mrs. Ball. The widow enjoyed company, but she didn't see as many people as she had done when they'd all shared the mayor's large home, now she had moved to the edge of town with Richard and Emily. Mrs. Ball would be grateful for the visit, Marta was sure of it.

She pulled on a clean, cotton nightgown, then fetched her writing desk and put it on the bed. She plumped the pillows and set them upright so she could lean against them, then untucked the sheets and blankets and slid under them before putting the writing desk on her lap. She opened up Mr. Groves' letter again and re-read it.

Dear Young Woman of Minnesota

I must confess that this is the first letter of its kind that I have ever written. I am not even sure why, other than a friend of mine seems determined to see me well-matched, and perhaps he is right that it is time to find the right young lady.

I am a cowboy. I say this now as I am not sure that my prospects rise any higher than that, but it is honest work and I do it well. It does mean many days, weeks, and even months away from home, which would make many women balk, no doubt, but it is strangely satisfying, bringing in a herd.

Because of my work, I spend many hours without much company, so I haven't had much time to develop interests outside of my work, though I do like to read and we occasionally sing a little around the fire. My friend, Nev, plays the mouth organ, and well, he's actually pretty good at it. Must be all the hours of practice he can get in without disturbing anyone but me and the cows.

I don't know what else to say, really. Just that I'm not looking for one of those girls that wants nothing more than to be a wife and mother. I love that you have work that you enjoy and would never wish to take that from you. And I can learn to dance if it is truly something that you must have!

Yours hopefully

Elias Groves

It was a nice letter, one that showed that this man had a sense of humor and was self-deprecating. Marta was sure that he had many stories and she would somehow find a way to coax them out of him, though she worried that it might be some time before she heard from him again if he was out on a cattle drive, somewhere. She dipped her pen into the inkwell and began to write a reply. She tried to keep her tone light, as he had done, though she couldn't help her passion for her work and her delight in her life in Iron Creek spilling over onto the page. She wondered if it might concern him that she did not want to leave the place she now called home but figured that it was best to find such things out before they grew close.

It took her four attempts to make the letter perfect, but once she had, she folded it neatly and addressed it to Mr.

Groves' address in New Mexico. After placing it on the dresser, she pulled the drapes against the late afternoon sunshine. She was almost too excited to go to sleep, so she lay on her back, looking up at the slightly rough spot on the ceiling above her bed, wondering what he looked like. She liked to think that he was dark haired with dark eyes, or perhaps blue eyes, swarthy skin from all the hours in the saddle, and strong, very strong like the heroes in her romance novels.

CHAPTER 5

*J*une 3, 1890, Camp Hill Ranch, New Mexico

Elias was surprised by how much he enjoyed working at the ranch. Both Nev and Mr. Hill seemed to respect his opinion, and he was being entrusted with more responsibilities every day. Nev, of course, was distracted by being a newlywed, and he spent more time with his new wife than he did out on the land where he should be. Elias didn't mind covering for him; without Nev, he'd not have a job, so he did his friend's work most days, too. But the more settled he felt at the ranch, the more unsettled he felt about his own future. Mr. Hill had been right when he'd said that there was a time in a man's life when what he has isn't enough and he begins to seek out more – and Elias knew that he did not want to just be a ranch hand for the rest of his days. He wanted his own ranch.

Yet he had no idea how he could ever achieve such a thing. Now he had regular work, he could start to save. His tastes were simple, and he didn't spend much money, but it would never be enough to buy the land and livestock he'd need. He'd need a miracle, but that miracle was unlikely to be found in the matrimonials column of the newspaper. A woman with a sizable dowry had no need to advertise for a husband; her father or brothers would already have her marriage planned for her. But that didn't mean he couldn't find love there. He'd written to a number of ladies and hoped that at least one of them would write back. Now, all he had to do was wait. And he was good at that. Years of herding cattle makes a man patient.

"Elias," Mr. Hill called out from his rocking chair on the deck. "Come on inside a minute."

Elias put down the ax by the woodpile he'd been chopping, took off his hat, wiped his brow with a handkerchief, and stepped up onto the deck. Mr. Hill smiled at him as he got up out of his chair.

"You work hard, I cannot deny that," the older man said approvingly.

"Is there something wrong?"

"No, not at all," Mr. Hill said. "Come on in."

They went inside the house and into Mr. Hill's study. It was a dark room; all the walls were paneled in mahogany that gleamed when Mr. Hill turned on the lamps. A small bookcase held no more than a dozen books. It reminded

Elias a little of Mr. Greenslade's home, where reading had been frowned upon. Mr. Hill pulled out a pile of papers from his desk.

"Elias, these are the deeds to the ranch. I've told Nev that I'll be leaving them with my lawyer in town should he ever need them, but the boy's got a brain as leaky as an old bucket, so I'm telling you. Everything he needs, should anything happen to me, will be locked up safely with Frederick Lawson. You hear me?"

"I hear you, Sir, but surely it's not something we need to worry about for some time yet? You're in fine health, are you not?"

"Doc's a bit concerned about my heart, but I'm fine," Mr. Hill said hurriedly. "But there's never any harm in being prepared. I know you'll keep an eye on my boy if you're still here."

"You make it sound as if you expect me to leave," Elias said.

"I think you've been discovering that you're more ambitious than you thought you were. And that's no bad thing. A man needs to be in charge of his own destiny, not reliant on someone else's charity. Though now you're here, I'd hate to see you go."

"Thank you, Sir. I know you had your reservations about me. I'm glad I've proved that I'm not what everyone thinks I am."

"Now, get back to work, before I change my mind," Mr.

Hill said with a grin. "Thank you. You've been good for Neville. He needed a steady influence."

"Ah, that'll be Millie, not me," Elias said humbly. "She's the one who's good for him."

"She's as silly and flighty as he is. No, you keep on showing him how to do his job. Then, if you do leave, perhaps he'll know how not to run the place into the ground." Elias turned to leave. "Oh, I almost forgot." Mr. Hill reached across his desk and picked up a letter. "This came for you earlier. Meant to give it to you after breakfast and forgot."

"Thank you, Sir," Elias said, taking the letter. He glanced at the handwriting on the envelope. It was neat and elegant, and there wasn't a single smudge. Then he looked at the return address. It must be from the interesting young lady in Minnesota, the one who had no intention of giving up her job and loved dancing. He opened it as he made his way back out into the yard.

Dear Mr. Groves

Thank you for your rather intriguing letter. Though you did not say much, you left me with a hundred questions I'd like to ask. However, I shall be kind and will only ask a few now. After all, we perhaps have the joys of a long correspondence ahead of us, when I shall undoubtedly ask the rest.

So, I shall start with the easiest ones. I need to get a picture of you in my mind, so I would be grateful if you would describe yourself. What color hair do you have? Is it curly or straight? And your eyes, what color are they? Are you tall, short, thin, fat? I am presuming that you are strong because of your work. I would imagine working with cattle needs considerable strength.

I am blonde, I have blue eyes, and I am usually covered in flour because I am a baker. Mostly, I wear my hair pinned up out of the way, but when I, very occasionally, get to wear it loose, it has a gentle wave to it. I am tall, and strong and I can lift large bags of flour from the miller's cart as easily as Wes, the man whose bakery I work in.

I find myself here in Iron Creek because a friend of mine recently moved here and I came along, too. I love the place. It is full of warm people, and none of them seems to mind that my work is the most important thing in the world to me. In truth, many of them seem to actively encourage me to devote myself to it even more!

The town is the perfect place, and it is growing so fast. We have our own railway station, a theater with its own theater troupe, the best-selling newspaper in all of Minnesota, and a fine medical clinic, where my friend Emily works. I never want to leave here, so if your hope is for a wife who will come to you, I am not the girl for you. I am also not the kind of woman who gives up everything to become a wife and mother. I know it is seen as unladylike to work, but I don't care. I am what I am.

Now, back to my questions for you. You said you are a cowboy and that you rarely stay in one place for long, so how will I be able to write to you if I do not know where you are? Should I expect long gaps between letters? If so, then I will not worry that you have already decided you hate me if I do not hear from you for a while.

And why did you write to me? Of all the people you could have written to, what made you reply to my advertisement?

Yours most interestedly

Marta Pauling

He couldn't help smiling. Her questions were those to be expected at this stage of their correspondence, but it was the way she wrote them. It was as if she were so excited that she could hardly stop the words from tumbling out. He was very glad that she, of all the women he had written to, had written back. There had been something about her advertisement, and he was pleased to see more of it in her letter. She had a zest for life and the things and people that she loved. That she had followed her best friend to live somewhere new told him a lot about her character. She was clearly adventurous and loyal.

He tucked the letter in his pocket and returned to chopping wood. It was one of those chores that helped get rid of any anxieties. The rhythmic swing of the ax and the satisfying thunk as it hit the wood and cleaved it in two. He worked solidly until there was enough wood split to last the bunkhouse and the ranch house for the next month, then stacked it neatly in each of the two woodsheds.

The light was fading, so he went inside and put some stew on the stove to cook, then sat on his bed and wrote a reply to Miss Pauling. He answered her questions as best he could and asked her a few of his own, then tried to imagine what she looked like. She had only told him pieces, but he put them together and felt sure that she was pretty. Not that he cared that much about a woman's looks. The women he'd cared for most in his life had not been what would be considered beautiful, but they had been lovely to him because of their strength and kindness.

"Hey, Elias, I'm going into town. Thought it might be nice to play some cards at the saloon. You interested?" Nev called as he banged on the door and barged his way into the bunkhouse without waiting to be told to come in. When you owned the place, you could do that.

"Not tonight," Elias said, feeling strangely uninterested in such entertainment. "But I hope you don't lose again. Millie will be furious if you do."

"I know, I know," Nev said distractedly. "But it's fun, and I don't see why she thinks I'll change my habits just because we are married. She didn't complain before we were married."

"I suppose she thought that perhaps with her to come home to every night, you'd not need other distractions. Or maybe she thought that you might actually grow up," Elias teased.

"Never," Nev said, looking comically aghast. "How

could anyone think that I would grow up? And I do love going home to her, but I want to do something else every now and again. Too much of a good thing soon becomes dull."

"I understand. Perhaps you should tell her that."

"The words always come out wrong when I try. But maybe you could tell her. She likes you and would listen to you, I'm sure of it."

"I'll think about it, but she's your wife," Elias said. "If you can't talk to her now, it's only going to get harder, Nev. You need to find a way."

Nev left Elias alone with his thoughts and Miss Pauling's letter. It fascinated him that she called herself a baker. He'd never known a woman baker, though he'd seen a few bakers' wives serving in bakery shops. He wondered if that was what she meant, that she worked in a bakery, but she had been quite definite, and from what he had read about her so far, he did not think that she was a woman to say anything she did not mean. She had been quite direct. To become a female baker really was something rather incredible.

He thought about his own life and wished he'd made more of it. He realized that he had used his inauspicious start as an excuse to not achieve anything, assuming that all doors would be closed to him even if he tried his best. He knew he could do more than he had done. He knew he was as good a man as any other, and better than most, yet he continued to punish himself for something that he had been given no choice about. It was time to stop doing that. It was time to forgive himself and start over. He was quick, clever, and hardworking – and he knew that both Mr. Hill and Nev needed him here and valued his work. If he could convince Mr. Hill of his worth, a man who had not wanted to give him the time of day when he'd first come to Camp Hill begging for work, he could convince others of it, too. He wanted a ranch of his own, and he would do whatever he could to make that happen.

CHAPTER 6

June 23, 1890, Iron Creek, Minnesota

Marta was frustrated. She glanced at the clock in the bakery kitchen for the hundredth time in less than an hour and sighed. She did not know why she felt so unsettled or why she was unable to lose herself in her work. Normally, baking was the only thing on her mind, but now she could barely concentrate on it enough to make the most basic items. She grabbed the rolling pin and began to roll out the pastry for the day's pies. She went at it so brutally that the pastry was too thin and tore. With a sigh, she rolled it back up into a ball and wrapped it in paper, then left it on the windowsill to cool before trying again.

"What is wrong with you recently?" Wes asked, passing by with a tray of loaves to go in the oven, as she stood at her work bench, shaking her head and trying to fight back tears.

"You're not yourself. I hoped you'd snap out of it over the weekend, perhaps talk it all over with Emily over your lunch with her on Sunday, but it's clear you haven't."

"I'm sorry," she said. "I only wish I knew. I've never felt this way before."

"If I didn't know better, I'd have thought you were in love," Wes joked. He put the loaves into the vast oven and came back to her bench. He looked at her, as if trying to figure out what was wrong, then pulled her into his arms. "Whatever it is, it isn't worth crying over."

"Oh, Wes, it's not that I'm in love. More that I fear I never will be," she wailed, the tears that she'd wanted to cry beginning to pour down her cheeks. "I put an advertisement in the newspapers, and there was only one reply that even vaguely interested me, and I've not heard anything more from him, and what if he doesn't write back? I know I'm not easy and docile and that few men want a woman like me, but surely there must be one, somewhere?"

Wes chuckled. "Oh, the wait for the letters. It is excruciating," he agreed.

"Would you have minded if Clarice wanted to work? If she hadn't wanted to move here?" she said, extricating herself from his arms. She pulled a handkerchief from the pocket of her apron, blew her nose loudly and wiped her eyes.

"It wasn't exactly our situation. She could hardly wait to get away from her home and her work." He grimaced, remembering Clarice's life before they were wed. "But I did accept her just as she was, and any man who truly loves you will do the same."

"Are you sure?" Marta asked desperately. He nodded and smiled at her. "But why do they not write?"

"When did you last write to him?"

"In mid-May. What if he doesn't write back?"

"Where is he?" Wes asked.

"In New Mexico."

"Then it'll be here soon enough. Remember, it takes time for a letter to get there and a response to come back. But if he's any kind of man, he'll see that you're a gem. He'll write back. A girl like you doesn't come around too often, and you're far more interesting than all those pale and silly dolls out there."

Marta gave him a wan smile. "Clarice is a lucky girl to have found you."

"And I am a lucky man to have her – and to have you working for me. I think of you as a sister, and I promise that I will not let anyone hurt you, ever." He paused and pulled a funny face that made her laugh. "Now, if you could knead the dough for the next batch of loaves, that would be wonderful. I think that I'd best take care of the pastry today, don't you?"

"I think that might be a good idea," she agreed.

Kneading the dough helped to get rid of much of her anxiety, but her mind kept straying towards the thought that no man wanted a woman who cared as much for her work as she did for the idea of becoming a mother or being a wife. How would she ever be able to explain that it wasn't that she didn't want those things but that she needed her work as well? Why were men permitted to have everything when women were not? It seemed dreadfully unfair to Marta. She was sure that she would not ever be the type to settle for a domestic life, even though it was all that was expected of her. She didn't care that tongues would wag or that she would be called unwomanly.

The rest of the day passed quickly. Wes checked on her more often than usual, which made her snap at him, even though she knew he was concerned for both her and his pastries. But he seemed not to mind. He truly was the brother she had never had, and she loved working with him. They closed the shop and pulled down the blinds together as they always did. Marta picked up the broom as Wes began to wipe down the sides.

"You deserve to have a share in the bakery," Wes said as if he was making a simple observation about the color and crispness of a loaf's crust.

"I'm sorry?" she said, stopping mid-sweep.

"The bakery. You are as much a part of it as I am. You work as hard. You have brought new recipes with you, and our success since you came has only grown. You deserve a share of that success, not just a wage."

"But I cannot offer you any money," she said. "I can't buy a share."

"I'm not expecting you to," he said with a smile. "You've earned your share with all you bring to the business. And I have big plans. I think we should open another shop, perhaps in Grand Marais."

"But I don't want to move to Grand Marais," she said, suddenly afraid he would take her away from the only place that had really felt like home to her and the people she loved.

"No, but Clarice does," he said with a smile. "She loves the lake and thinks that the school there is better than the one here. I've tried to tell her that the Iron Creek one is just as good, but women when they are pregnant have their whims, and I, as her loving husband, must obey. I was thinking you could run the bakery here."

"But that means we wouldn't be working together," Marta said, feeling almost deserted even though nothing had even been agreed upon.

"My intention would be that either I come here once a month or you come to Grand Marais, or perhaps both, so we can try out new recipes and decide upon the products together. We can go over the accounts and other business matters and have lunch or supper together. I know that Clarice will need to hear all the gossip from here, and I am terrible at remembering everything."

It struck Marta again just how lucky Clarice was to have a man who loved her as much as Wes did, one who was prepared to change his entire life if it meant it would make her happy. "What if she changes her mind?"

"Then I come back, we work together, and I find another baker to take over the Grand Marais bakery, though I can't imagine I'll find another one as good as you. Or perhaps we arrange to deliver the bread and pastries from here to there each day, so we don't need to find a baker, just an excellent shop manager."

"You've really thought about all of this," she said, stunned by everything he'd just said. "I am flattered that you would trust me with one of the bakeries and that you want me to be such a big part of your plans for the future."

"But?" Wes asked, sensing there was something more coming.

"But I don't know anything about running a bakery," she said.

"Of course you do. From all Emily told me about when you were in Boston, you ran that place for that fool of a man you worked for."

"He wasn't a fool," Marta said. "Just a little lazy. But he was kind and let me do what I wanted, so I didn't mind."

"He was a fool because he let you go, which has been entirely to my benefit."

"So, you are not a fool?" Marta teased him.

"Only sometimes," he said with a grin. "Think about it. I would be happy to offer you thirty-five percent of the business. As you say, you don't have the money to invest right now, so you can't contribute to the cost of the buildings or the ovens and such like, but you'll be doing everything else the same as me. Once we've made enough profit to pay me back for those outlays, we'll split everything down the middle."

"I'll think about it." She started to sweep the floor again, her mind racing, then stopped. "You've said this even though I admitted that I want to find a husband. Are you not afraid that I'll want to leave if I do?"

"Not in the slightest," Wes said with a grin. "You'll not give up your work – you love it too much – and no man who loves you would ever ask you to. Our conversation this morning told me everything I needed to know to be sure that you want to be here."

Marta left the bakery intending to go straight home, but she decided to go and visit Emily instead. She had too much on her mind to try to sift through it all alone. It was a lovely warm day and the late spring flowers in the meadows by the side of the road danced in the gentle breeze as she made her way up to the Balls' new home. Emily was in the front yard, taking in her washing.

"Good afternoon, married lady," Marta said. She hurried forward and helped Emily fold the last bed sheet before putting it in the basket.

"What are you doing here?" Emily asked. "I didn't expect to see you again until next Sunday, at church."

"Well, I have something I should have told you about

yesterday and something else that came up today. I just need to talk it all through."

Emily nodded. "Of course. You can tell me anything."

They went into the kitchen. Marta sat at the kitchen table while Emily made them each a cup of tea and cut them each a slice of cake. "Your apple spice cake is Richard's favorite," Emily said, handing Marta hers as she took a seat at the table. "Now, tell me everything."

Marta did. She started with the proposition that Wes had just made. It seemed the easier of the two matters to discuss. Emily stared at her wide-eyed. "But that is such excellent news. I know he values you, but this is real proof of just how much."

"You think I should do it?" Marta asked.

"I absolutely do," Emily said excitedly. "Your own bakery to run as you see fit. I cannot think of anything more perfect for you. And how exciting that Clarice is expecting a child. How happy they must be. I am sad to hear that Clarice and Wes will be leaving town, though. I'm very fond of them both."

"It is exciting. Wes thinks she may change her mind once they move and the baby comes, that she'll miss their friends and the support they have here, but he's thought about that eventuality, too. Either way, I'd have a share in the business, forever."

"You are going to say yes to him, aren't you?" Emily asked a little anxiously.

"I am," Marta said slowly. "I should have accepted before I left, but I wanted to talk it over with you and see what you thought."

"I fail to see what my thoughts on the matter bring. I've never known you to be so happy as you are working in the bakery. I would have been disappointed in you if you'd said no to being a real and permanent part of it. I shall be so proud to see your name above the door every time I walk past."

"And come inside, I hope," Marta said with a grin. "I shall ensure there is always something delicious for you."

"Thank you," Emily said, grinning. "Now, what is the other matter?"

"Men," Marta said bluntly.

"Men?" Emily asked, looking puzzled.

"Writing to men. Do you truly think it is possible to find a man by correspondence who'll truly respect all the things we've just discussed? My work is so important to me that I cannot imagine ever giving it up."

"Richard has no qualms about me working. Andy and Amy work together, Dr. Anna works, and Alec does not mind, and all of them met through the matrimonials. Many men are not concerned by such things, Marta." She paused for a moment. "You've already written to someone?"

"Well, no, but yes. I placed an advertisement and several men who were totally unsuitable wrote back to me. There was one, and he didn't seem to mind one bit, but he's not written back."

"Give it time. A letter will come. One may even be waiting for you at my father's house when you return. It is possible to find someone who is perfect by correspondence, but you are going to have to be uncharacteristically patient, my dear friend."

CHAPTER 7

*J*une 24, 1890, Iron Creek, Minnesota

Marta had fretted less at work after her talks with both Wes and Emily. Her mind was clearer, at least about what her future in Iron Creek would hold. Wes had been delighted that she had accepted his offer, and they had celebrated with cake and coffee at the end of the working day. She'd gone back home feeling that at least one part of her life was going as well as it possibly could. Her heart began to race when she saw the letter with Mr. Groves' handwriting on the envelope propped up on the hall table. She ripped it open and began to read as she went upstairs to her room.

Dear Miss Pauling,

I am so glad that you wrote back to me. Your letter brightened my day immeasurably. And I do not mind your questions one bit, so please ask as many as you like. I will tell you if I cannot answer or am perhaps not ready to answer an inquiry yet.

Firstly, you wished to know of my appearance. I am taller than most men I've met but, thought this may sound strange, I am not too tall. What I mean by that, is that I am not gangly like my friend Nev who is a good few inches taller than me. I like to think I am well-proportioned, and you are right to assume that I am strong. Carrying calves around and getting stubborn bulls to go where you want them to is harder work than many might think. I have dark hair that tends to get mussed easily, though is neither straight nor curly. And I have green eyes, which I know is a rather unusual combination.

Your town sounds lovely. Perhaps one day, if we continue to write to one another, I might come and visit you there. I would like to go to the theater and see a play. I've never done so, but it sounds interesting. Nev went once, in Santa Fe. He said it was strange that he completely forgot that the men and women on the stage were actors because he was utterly caught up in the story. I feel that way when I read, so I am sure I would be the same seeing those stories in front of me that way.

I am currently working at a ranch on the borders of New Mexico and Colorado. It's owned by Nev's father, and I can thank Nev for my position here. Mr. Hill did not think too much of me as just an itinerant cowboy until I started driving his cattle with Nev. So, in answer to your question about how often I'll be able to write, I'll not leave you waiting any longer than necessary for a reply, though I know the mail can take a while. There are a couple of times a year when we're away from the ranch, taking the cattle to market and bringing new ones back, but I'll let you know about that, so you don't fret.

And I wrote to you because you seemed to know who you are and what you want. I liked that. Now, if I may be so bold, I'd be glad to ask you why you wrote back to me? And tell me about your bakery and all the delicious things you make there.

Yours most eagerly

Elias Groves

It was a wonderful letter, even if it was a little short. He had signed himself as eager and wanted to know more about her. Marta sighed happily as she opened her bedroom door and went inside. She pulled out her writing desk, sat on the bed, and sucked at the end of her pen wondering what to write. After some thought, she dipped the pen in the ink and began to write. She was amazed to find it was easy to write to him if she just wrote down what she'd say if they were talking face to face. She didn't know anything about the man, really, yet she felt peculiarly close to him. She wondered if other people in Iron Creek had felt the same way when they'd been writing to one another. She knew that it hadn't been that way for Emily and Richard, but that was because they had come together rather differently, though it had all begun with an advertisement.

Happy that she had told Mr. Groves everything he had asked, and some things he had not, and that she had asked him plenty of questions of her own, she addressed the envelope and hurried down the stairs and out onto the street. Sheriff Hansen was sitting on the porch of the sheriff's office. He tipped his hat and smiled at her.

"Good day," she called to him as she passed by.

She reached the postal office as Hank Wilson was about to lock the front door. "Oh, Mr. Wilson, I am so glad I caught you in time," she said. "I need to send this to New Mexico immediately."

Mr. Wilson glanced at the envelope and grinned. "Do we have another budding romance?" he asked. Marta felt her cheeks flush, which only made his smile wider.

"I don't know," she admitted, knowing that the news would be all over town by the morning. Hank was a terrible gossip. "But I'd like to find out."

"Well, you come on in. I'll not stand in the way of young love," Mr. Wilson said opening the door and ushering her inside. He went behind the counter, calculated the postage, and took Marta's coins. "I may even catch the train in time to get this in with all the other mail going through Duluth."

"Thank you."

They went back outside, and he locked the door of the postal office before hurrying off toward the station. Marta prayed he made it in time. She wanted Mr. Groves to receive her letter as quickly as possible.

Marta didn't often have time to saunter along Main Street, but she did so as she made her way home. She peered into the windows of the new dress shop that had opened up. She wondered how much trade they got; everyone in Iron Creek tended to get their clothes made by Mrs. Cable. She'd had to take on an apprentice as demand had grown, but she was still too busy. Perhaps a new dressmaker in town was a good thing, and the floral gown in the window was lovely. Marta couldn't help imagining what it would look like on her, but she could not afford a new dress this month, so she turned away.

As she walked on, she saw Mrs. Cable and Nelly Graham talking outside the clinic. Feeling a little guilty for having liked the look of the floral dress, she hurried across the road to join them. "I was just looking," she said quickly.

"She makes nice dresses," Mrs. Cable said with an understanding smile. "You don't need to feel bad for me. I've more work than I know what to do with. I'll need an experienced seamstress and a new apprentice to keep up with it. If she can ease my workload just a little, I'll be grateful. And we've spoken, Mrs. Halfon and me. She's a nice lady, doesn't want to tread on my toes."

"I'm glad," Marta said. She turned to Nelly "And how is Emily getting on at the clinic? She loves working with you."

"She is a delight. She's a natural nurse who puts

everyone at ease. I'll be happy to stop work one day, knowing she's there in my place."

"I'm glad," Marta repeated.

"And I hear that there will be a new sign above the bakery soon," Mrs. Cable said, giving Marta a knowing look. "Wes told me all about him offering you part of the bakery and his and Clarice's plans to move to Grand Marais."

"It is both very exciting and extremely daunting," Marta said. "I don't know if I will be able to uphold Wes' standards, but I am going to do my best."

"You're as fine a baker as he is, if not better," Nelly said firmly. "That wedding cake you made for Emily and Richard was the finest thing I have ever eaten."

"Thank you." Marta found herself blushing again at the compliment. "I should get back. I have to make dinner for Mayor Winston."

The women said their goodbyes, and Marta went home. Mayor Winston was in his study, working on something for the town. She poked her head around the door to let him know she was home, then went into the kitchen. The familiar actions of scrubbing and peeling the vegetables for the casserole and then preparing the meat to roast were comforting. She felt the excitement and nervousness she'd been feeling for days begin to dissipate. He had written to her, and he wanted to know more about her. Perhaps he was the one, perhaps he was not, but at least they would have the chance to find out.

July 8, 1890, Camp Hill Ranch, New Mexico

"Letter for you, Elias," Nev said, coming into the bunkhouse. "Nice handwriting. You writing to someone fancy? Did you take my advice to find a wife, after all?"

Elias snatched the letter from Nev and found it hard to suppress a smile when he saw it was from Miss Pauling. "None of your business, Nev," he said, tucking the letter in his pocket.

"Dad wants us to take the steers to market in Aztec. Can you be ready in an hour?"

"Sure, I'll be ready," Elias assured him.

"No getting distracted, my friend," Nev teased as he let himself out. Elias waited. Once he was sure Nev was gone and not coming back, he pulled out the letter and began to read.

Dear Mr. Groves,

I am so glad that my letter brought you pleasure. I can definitely tell you that yours made me very happy, too, though it seemed to take an age to arrive. I do hope you won't have to go on very long cattle drives or I shall be half out of my mind by the time your next letter reaches me.

Now, you wanted to know why I chose to write to you, of

all the replies to my advertisement. Well, that is quite simple. You sounded interesting. The others were dull or ignored everything I asked for. Most of them seemed to think that a wife belongs in the home, raising babies and caring for her man, not pursuing her own interests, so that ruled them out. You didn't seem to mind that I love my work. And you are a cowboy rather than a miserable clerk.

As to my baking, I could talk about food forever and never get bored. There is nothing more important to me. And it should be to everyone. After all, we cannot survive without food. Why should that food be as dull as most people's lives? It should be full of hope and excitement, perhaps then people might find more happiness in this world. I try to bring a little pleasure to the people I care about, one bite at a time.

But I shall no longer be employed at the bakery. I have the most exciting news. Wes, my employer, offered me the opportunity to become his partner and run the Iron Creek bakery on my own. He and his wife wish to move to Grand Marais and open a new bakery there. They want to be by the lake, so I get my own bakery! I can hardly believe it. To think a girl like me, who truly started with absolutely nothing, will actually have a part-share in my own bakery is unbelievable and yet it is real!

Working with Wes is a delight. He is as obsessed as I am. We recently developed a new recipe, and everyone in town loves it. We can't make enough of it, and it sells out every single day. But they also love his French-inspired recipes.

He was trained by a wonderful Frenchman who I hope to meet someday. Wes assures me that I will and that he won't stay away when he opens the new bakery in Grand Marais.

You speak of Nev often in your letters. I presume he is your closest friend? And he is the son of your employer? Does that not make things a little difficult sometimes? I know I often forget that Wes is my employer as he is like an older brother to me. I am glad that we are now almost equals in the running of the business as it makes things much easier.

My dearest friend is Emily. She is training to become a nurse and is married to the town lawyer, though all three of us came here from Boston. They have completely rebuilt a beautiful old house on the edge of town. I currently live in her father's house. He's the mayor and the kindest man I think I've ever known. Every Sunday, we all go to church and then to Emily's for lunch. Emily and I met at church in Boston and shared a little cottage for a time before she met Richard.

I am not sure what else to tell you other than that I cannot wait for your next letter and I hope that you are well.

Yours most excitedly

Marta Pauling

Elias wrote a quick reply. He knew he didn't really have the time to do so, but he didn't want to have to wait until he reached Aztec to mail it to her. Miss Pauling had made it quite clear that she did not enjoy the wait for his letters as it was, so to delay it any further seemed cruel. He would ask Mr. Hill to mail it for him when he next went into town.

When he had finished, he made his way to the paddock and whistled for Jet, who trotted toward him. Elias patted the animal's neck as he slipped a halter over his head, then led him out of the paddock to the stable, where he rubbed him down and put on a saddle and a bridle. He tied his bedroll to the back of the saddle, then took his saddlebags to the back of the ranch house, where Mrs. Rawlings, the Hills' housekeeper, had left food, water, and cooking utensils out on the back porch for him and Nev.

He rapped on the back door and let himself inside. Mrs. Rawlings emerged from the kitchen. "You got all you need?" she asked.

"Yes, thank you," he said. "But I need to mail this letter as soon as possible. I think Mr. Hill said he was going into town tomorrow. Can you give it to him, please?"

"Sure I can, Elias. Is this the young lady that Neville told me about?" she teased, taking the letter and looking at the address on it.

"That man is a worse gossip than any woman," Elias said, trying to hide his annoyance that even this had become public knowledge.

"He's just excited for you. Wants you to be as happy as he and Millie are."

"I know. I know. I just wish he'd let me find out for sure if I might be before he told everyone," Elias said.

"You take your time, Elias," she warned him. "It's best to be sure before you do something you can't undo. She'll be a lucky girl to have a man like you."

"Even with my past?"

"Your past is in the past, boy. Let it rest there. She needs to know the man you are, not the boy you were."

With her words of advice ringing in his ears, Elias headed back out to the yard. Nev was already on horseback, so Elias untied Jet and mounted up. The two men rode out of the yard, toward the cattle pens. Nev leaned down and opened the gate, and Elias and Jet moved into the pen and began to urge the steers out. They were soon on their way, crossing terrain they knew well. The market in Aztec was a regular drive to sell their steers when it grew too expensive to raise them further.

"Dad wants me to look for a new bull while we're there, though he thinks it may be better to wait until we go to Colorado Springs in the fall."

"If Uriah Hanley's there, he had a bull he was looking to sell. Good pedigree and has sired some good cattle. If you can get a good price, I doubt there'd be a better animal for the ranch."

"I didn't know Hanley was selling his bull. That would be an animal Dad would be happy with. I just hope I can get him to agree to a price Dad would be happy with. The two of them are as stubborn as each other."

"That they are," Elias agreed.

CHAPTER 8

*J*uly 12, 1890, Grand Marais, Minnesota

It had taken Wes remarkably little time to get his family settled in a neat little house near the lake in Grand Marais and the new bakery ready for its grand opening. Marta was so excited. Half of Iron Creek had come to Grand Marais to celebrate with them, and Wes' mentor had come with his wife. Madame Lancelot, it turned out, was responsible for the recipes for many of Marta's favorite dishes, but Monsieur Lancelot was an artist. Working with him to prepare everything for the opening day had been an honor and a pleasure.

"You are even more talented than Wesley," Madame Lancelot said with a smile as she tasted some of Marta's pastries.

Marta glanced at Wes anxiously, hoping he had not taken

offense at the French lady's comment. He grinned at her. "I was a lucky man the day she decided to move to Iron Creek," he agreed.

"I've never known anyone 'ave such a light touch," Monsieur Lancelot said.

"I think it is because my hands are always cold," Marta said. "The butter doesn't melt until the pastries are in the oven."

"You may 'ave a point there," Monsieur Lancelot said. "The man I learned from in France when I was a boy, 'e also 'ad cold 'ands, and the pastries were *magnifique*." He kissed his fingers and closed his eyes for a moment. A look of pleasure spread over his wrinkled face. It was as if he was tasting the pastries all over again.

They each took a tray of breads, cakes, pies, and other delights out into the shop. Marta put them out on the counter while Wes opened the shop door. Emily, Richard, and Mayor Winston were the first through the door, and Marta was glad to see them. Behind them were some unfamiliar faces. Wes and Clarice introduced themselves to their new neighbors while Marta and the Lancelots encouraged everyone to try the breads and pastries. Everyone bought at least a loaf of bread and a cake to take home with them, and everything was sold out before midday. The opening had been a great success.

Reluctantly, they bade farewell to their guests. Wes kissed his wife and sent her home to rest, then insisted that the Lancelots go to their boarding house, where he and Clarice would meet them for dinner later. Exhausted, they closed the door of the bakery. "I shall miss you," Marta said as she and Wes fell into their cleaning routine. "I shall have to do all the cleaning myself."

"Take on a girl to work in the shop," Wes said. "I have Clarice to help me, but you can be sure that I will be hiring someone once she tells me that her belly is too big for her to be on her feet all day."

"I shall. There's bound to be someone in town who would like to work somewhere where they get free bread each day," Marta joked.

"I think many would give up the jobs they already have," Wes agreed with a laugh.

"Things are going to go well for you here. It's a good spot, right in the heart of the town. Lots of people came, and I didn't see a single unhappy face as they tried everything. They'll be back."

"I do hope so. Clarice seems happy here," Wes said. "I'm going to miss everyone in Iron Creek, though."

"Come and visit us often," Marta said. She put down the broom and took off her apron. "And I will see you in a fortnight so we can discuss how things are going."

He hugged her tightly. "I shall miss working with you. Madame Lancelot is right; you are a better baker than all of us."

"Not better than Monsieur Lancelot," Marta said, shaking her head.

"Better than Anton," Wes said with a grin. "Madame thinks I am better than him, so if you are better than me, you must be better than him."

"She said that? I hope not to his face," Marta said with a gasp.

"She did. She is a frank and honest Frenchwoman."

"When did she say it?"

"When he was trying to convince me to stay and work for him. He was not happy about me leaving and said he had more to teach me. She pointed out that I had far outdone him for months. His French pride was stung for a while, but he agreed that she was right."

"But I'm not better than you, and you aren't better than him – we're just all a little different," Marta said, feeling very uncomfortable with such high praise.

"Accept the truth, Marta. You are brilliant. Possibly the best I will ever know. Keep doing what you do, you'll only get better."

Marta made her way to the inn where Emily, Richard, and Mayor Winston were waiting for her. "Wes said I am better than him, better than Monsieur Lancelot," she said, still stunned by what Wes had said.

"Of course you are," Emily said as if it were the most obvious thing in the world. "Now, do you want to eat before we go or shall we just get home and eat there?"

"I think I am too tired, too excited, too amazed to eat now," Marta said.

"I ate too much at the bakery," Mayor Winston confided. "So, shall we go home?"

"Let's," Richard said.

Mayor Winston's carriage was waiting for them with fresh horses from the public stable. Richard heaved himself up onto the driver's perch while Mayor Winston held the door open for Emily and Marta. Once they had clambered inside and gotten comfortable, Richard clicked to the horses and the carriage began to roll forwards. Marta was so tired that she fell asleep with her head on Emily's shoulder, almost all the way back to Iron Creek.

"We're home," Emily said, shaking Marta gently as they pulled into Iron Creek. Marta unwillingly opened her eyes, stretched a little, and sat upright. "Seeing how tired you are, perhaps we can have dinner together tomorrow instead of tonight?"

"I am so tired," Marta admitted. "All I want to do is sleep."

"I bought some pies," Mayor Winston said. "We'll not starve."

"We shall see you both at church in the morning," Emily said. "We'll bring the carriage back then."

JULY 12, 1890, Aztec, New Mexico

The market was busy. Elias was being careful to keep his head down, so he stayed in the boarding house out of the way, just watching from the window that overlooked the market square. There were too many ranchers in New Mexico who hadn't forgotten his past, even though he wanted them to. He'd worked for men all over the state, but few had wanted him for more than a short-handed cattle drive. He didn't want to make things harder for Nev. They needed to sell the steers, and they had to get a good price for Hanley's bull.

Nev had managed to get one of the best pens in a spot that everyone had to walk by. A few men stopped to talk to him about the animals, and some even got into the pen to look more closely at them. They were good steers with good bloodlines. Elias had no concerns that they would sell for a good price at the auction. The Hanley bull was just a few pens along. He was a fine animal with a broad back and strong legs. Elias watched Nev speaking with Uriah Hanley. His best chance of securing the bull would be to give Uriah a good price before the auction started so nobody else had a chance to pay more than Mr. Hill was willing to pay, but it wasn't looking good for Nev. Uriah turned away from him, looking angry.

The auction began just after noon, and the steers would be up shortly after that. Elias watched as four calves were sold for less than he would have expected and a cow in calf went for much more. Sometimes you could judge the mood of the crowd and guess quite accurately how much animals would sell for, but it seemed to be one of those days when predictions were almost impossible to make. When it was his turn, Nev led the animals into the auction pen. There was a large crowd around the pen, and that boded well. Elias watched men raising hands or fingers to each rising price. When the auctioneer closed the sale, Nev looked pleased. Elias breathed a sigh of relief.

Nev handed the steers to their new owner and took his cash from the auctioneer. He made a big to-do about leaving, making sure that Uriah Hanley saw him go. Hanley glared at him but didn't move. It looked like they were going to need to look for a bull in Colorado Springs at the fall auctions after all, but just as Nev was about to leave the marketplace, a boy caught up to him and tugged at his coat. Nev looked down at the lad, who led him back to the bull's pen, where Hanley grudgingly accepted Nev's money.

Elias and Nev celebrated in the saloon that night. Nev was over the moon that he'd be taking such a fine animal back for his father and that he'd managed to get a better price than he'd expected for the steers. Mr. Hill was going to be very happy with his son.

"I'm sorry you weren't there to see Uriah eat his words," Nev said happily. "I've always hated that man, but that bull is the finest I've seen in New Mexico in years."

"He threw me off his ranch, once," Elias admitted. "I

went for a job and told him the truth about my past. I think it was the first place I went to after Greenslade threw me off his land. He and Hanley were tight. He knew all about me and wasn't having me anywhere near his cows."

"He's a miserable old man. You were better off not getting a place there."

"I'm sorry I wasn't able to be much help today," Elias said, taking a gulp of beer.

"I know there are too many men down there that don't think anything of you. Please do not take this the wrong way, my friend, but have you thought any more about what we talked about when we were on the drive? In New Mexico, Colorado, and even Utah, your past is always going to catch you up. I don't want you to leave, but don't you think you'd be happier somewhere far away from all these miserable old men?"

"Maybe," Elias admitted.

"Is that why you're writing to Miss Pauling?" Nev asked. "Minnesota is a long way from here. You'd be able to start afresh."

"In part. I looked in the newspapers after we got back to Camp Hill, like you suggested. I thought about putting in my own advertisement but then realized that women were asking for what they wanted. I wrote to a few. Some of them wrote back, but I soon realized they weren't for me. But Miss Pauling, she's different. She's not like anyone I've ever known. She doesn't let anything stop her, not tradition, not expectations. She just gets on with living her life her way. I'd like to have some of her gumption."

"Sounds like she's just what you need," Nev said. "Why aren't you there already?"

"I'm waiting for her to say she wants me to go."

Nev chuckled. "Where's your gumption, my friend? If you want her, if you want a different life, a better life, you have to get out there and make it happen."

"When she says she wants me. I'll not force myself upon her," Elias said firmly. "I don't want to scare her away, and I need to find a way to tell her who I really am first. She needs to be able to make that choice knowing everything."

"Then tell her, and soon," Nev said. "Don't lose her because you waited too long."

CHAPTER 9

*J*uly 16, 1890, Iron Creek, Minnesota

It was strange unlocking the doors to a cold and empty bakery each morning. Marta missed Wes more than she could have possibly imagined. But she was determined not to let him down, so she worked harder than ever to make sure the bakery ran as smoothly as it had when they were both there. By Tuesday, she was exhausted from doing the work of three people, so she decided that it was time to put up a notice in the window, asking for help in the shop.

It had barely been up for half an hour when Gertie Flitwick came in and asked for the job. Marta was delighted. The Flitwicks were new to Iron Creek. Mr. Flitwick was a reporter and worked at the newspaper. His daughter Gertie was seventeen, pretty, and polite. Marta told her to come in this morning for a trial, and she had been pleasantly surprised to see how hardworking she was.

"You're hired," she said to the girl as they cleaned the shop together.

"I am?" Gertie said happily. "Mom will be so happy. I think I've been driving her half mad with worry since we got here. There didn't seem to be any work for a girl like me. I'm not good with a needle. I know that both Mrs. Cable and the new dress shop are looking for more apprentices, but I'd be terrible at that. The only thing I've ever been any good at is cooking."

"You're a good cook?" Marta asked. Gertie nodded. "Show me."

They went into the kitchen, and Marta told Gertie to use whatever she wanted to make something. Gertie looked a little scared at first, but she calmed down once she got into the larder and started to choose her ingredients, and she actually started humming to herself as she peeled and chopped the vegetables and added butter to a pan. Before long, the smell of onions cooking filled the bakery, making Marta feel hungry. Gertie added beef and browned it before adding carrots, celery, and a generous helping of stout. She tasted the gravy at odd moments throughout. Finally, she added some diced kidneys, seasoning, and herbs, then tasted it one final time and left it to cool while she made some pastry, which she left to cool on the windowsill before rolling it out.

She lined a pie tin with the pastry and baked it blind,

then added the steak and kidney filling and covered it with more pastry. She cracked an egg and brushed it over the top to make the pastry shine, then snipped a hole in the center to let the steam out before putting it in the oven. The smell was heavenly as it cooked. Marta could hardly wait to eat it, so much so that she almost burned her mouth when she took the first bite. The meat was tender and succulent, the gravy rich and delicious. The pastry was good but could be better, but that was something she could teach Gertie. The important thing was, the girl could cook and she had an excellent palate.

"Would you like to learn how to be a baker?" she asked the girl.

Gertie stared at her wide-eyed. "You think I could?"

"I think you could. It means very early mornings, and you'll never get to stay up late ever again, but it is a job that is worth every sacrifice," Marta said enthusiastically. "Go home and talk about it with your mother and father. There is no need to rush the decision, you'll have the job in the shop whatever you choose."

"Thank you," Gertie gushed before almost running out of the door.

Marta smiled, wrapped up the pie, and took it home with her. Mayor Winston would enjoy it very much. She hadn't expected to find someone who would want to learn bakery skills or who had such an aptitude. Gertie worked methodically, tidily, and with real consideration of the ingredients. It had been impressive to watch her work. Marta really hoped that she would accept her offer. She hadn't ever really considered teaching what she knew to anyone else, but she really wanted to now.

Mayor Winston was out on town business when she got home, but there was a letter from Mr. Groves on the hall table. She put the pie in the kitchen and took her letter into the parlor to read. It was the perfect addition to what had been an unexpectedly brilliant day.

Dear Miss Pauling

I am writing this rather hurriedly as I have to drive some steers to market. It isn't far away, but I wanted to be sure that you would not have to wait too long for a reply from me. I shall write more when I get back.

I am delighted to hear your news. I can tell how excited you are about it, and I look forward to you telling me more about it in your next letter. It must be a little daunting being in charge, but I am sure you will rise to the challenges ahead.

And you are right that Nev is my friend as well as my employer (of sorts). He is a good man and probably my only real friend. We find it works well because I know what I am doing and he happily takes my advice!

I am afraid that I must go now, but please write and tell me all about your bakery. I promise I will write more when I return from Aztec in a fortnight's time.

Yours most happily

Elias Groves

Marta smiled. He had obviously taken her words to heart and understood that she would worry if she did not hear from him, and such care for her made her like him even more. Such concern for her feelings told her that he was a good man. She barely knew him, and letters could be deceiving, but he had not needed to send this letter, and yet he had. She wondered if it would be too forward to ask him to come to Iron Creek in her next letter. She did not wish to scare him away, but she would never know if he would come if she didn't ask.

She decided to talk it over with Emily, so she headed to the clinic. Nelly Graham greeted her warmly. "It is lovely to see you, Marta, but she's not in today. She was up all night with a gentleman with a badly broken leg. Poor man is in a lot of pain. She'll probably be at home, tucked up in bed if she's any sense."

"Thank you, Mrs. Graham,"

"Call me Nelly, love, like everyone else does," Nelly insisted.

"Thank you, I shall," Marta said. "I'll take a chance and walk out to see her. Perhaps she'll be waking up and needing something to eat. I have a nice pie and a cherry *clafoutis* in the bakery. That'll save her having to cook tonight."

"That would be a great help to her, I'm sure."

Marta liked the walk to Emily's house, especially on a warm afternoon when the birds were singing and the meadow flowers were a riot of blues, yellows, pinks, purples, and reds. She picked some flowers as she walked, adding them to the basket of goodies she'd taken from the bakery. They would look lovely in the vase that Nelly had bought for Emily and Richard as a wedding gift.

The house was quiet when Marta arrived, though the washing line was full. Marta stepped up onto the deck and peered in through the window to see if Emily was up. She didn't want to wake her if she was sleeping. She jumped back when a pair of eyes stared back at her out of the kitchen window. Moments later, Richard appeared on the deck.

"I thought it was you," he said with a smile.

"I didn't want to wake Emily if she was sleeping. Nelly said she had a difficult night."

"She did, and she is," Richard said quietly. "I'd not wake her; she'll be terribly grumpy if you do."

"Not to worry," Marta said. "What are you doing home from work?"

"I have nothing to work on, so I thought I would come back and do some of Emily's chores for her, so she need not fret over them when she wakes."

"You did the laundry?" she asked, pointing at the line full of shirts and sheets.

"I did," he said. "Aunt Mary raised me to be a man who knows how to help around the house, and that's just as well as she's off with her new friends most days."

"I'm glad she did," Marta said with a grin. "Too many

men think it is women's work and that they don't need to lift a finger. I believe she has had lunch with the mayor every day this week." The two of them grinned. Both Mrs. Ball and Mayor Winston had taken some convincing that it would be perfectly proper to enjoy their friendship, but they were almost inseparable now. "Mayor Winston has been coming home with a huge grin on his face. It's rather sweet."

"I keep teasing Aunt Mary about wedding bells," Richard said as they went inside. "I know she has not long lost my uncle, but I know he would want her to be happy."

Suddenly, Marta remembered the basket in her hands and offered it to him. "I brought these." He took it and peered inside, then smiled.

"Our favorites. You are too good to us," he said happily. "But I'm sure you didn't walk all this way just to bring us these."

"No, I did not. I hoped to ask her advice on something, but it is of no matter. I can see her another day."

"Marta, is there something I can help you with? I'm not Emily, but I am told that I give good advice," Richard said earnestly. "I can make us a cup of coffee and we can enjoy a piece of that fruit cake I saw nestling in your basket."

Feeling a little self-conscious, Marta took a seat at the kitchen table and watched Richard prepare the coffee and slice the cake. She wasn't used to having men wait on her. She'd liked Richard from the start, and she liked him even more every time she saw him or learned something new about him. Emily was a very lucky girl.

"So, tell me everything," he said. He sat down opposite her and began stirring sugar into his cup.

She told him about the letters she had received from Mr. Groves and that he seemed to be a good man. Richard was a very good listener, and he didn't interrupt or hurry her. "And I suppose I want to know if a man would be offended to receive an invitation to come and meet me," she finished.

"Hmm," Richard said, scratching his chin thoughtfully. "Well, I cannot tell you how I would have felt in the circumstances you describe, but I like to think that I would have been delighted to receive an invitation to meet Emily had we been in a similar situation."

"But you are not like most men. You do laundry and cook," Marta pointed out, and they both laughed.

"I do," he said. "But when it comes to the thought of a pretty woman telling me she likes me, I'm much the same as most men. We struggle to know because young ladies are raised not to be too forward and so don't ever let us know. We don't need subtle hints. Men's brains are about as subtle as a kick to the head. Tell us directly. I can assure you that he will be glad you did."

His advice went so completely against everything that Marta had ever been told that it actually made perfect sense to her. Why waste time hinting about her feelings? Life was short enough and losing time with someone you cared for because of silly rules about how a woman should behave had never seemed sensible to her. "So you think I should write and invite him here?"

"I do," Richard confirmed. "We will gladly put him up if he cannot afford to stay at the hotel or if Nelly has no room at her place. That way, we can keep an eye on him and be sure that he is good enough for you." He was teasing, but Marta knew that her friends would indeed do all they could to make sure she was safe. It was like having a family, and she was very grateful for it.

"Then it is decided," she said. Though a sudden burst of butterflies in her belly told her that she still wasn't entirely sure, but she was determined not to let her nerves get in the way. She had to know what he was really like before she grew any more attached to the idea of him. "I shall invite Mr. Groves to visit us here in Iron Creek."

CHAPTER 10

*J*uly 30, 1890, Camp Hill Ranch, New Mexico

A large black carriage with a golden crest on the door drove into the yard and stopped outside the ranch house. Elias knew he had seen it somewhere before but couldn't quite place it.

"What's Uriah Hanley doing here?" Nev asked.

"That's Hanley's carriage?" Elias stared at the crest. Of course it was. He'd seen it when Hanley had visited Mr. Greenslade many years ago.

Uriah Hanley got out of the carriage and looked around, his expression disdainful, as if Camp Hill wasn't good enough for him. Elias looked down when the curmudgeonly rancher glared their way before marching up onto the deck and hammering on the door with his clenched fist.

"You didn't shortchange him on the bull, did you?" Elias asked Nev once he'd gone inside.

"I'm offended you think I would do such a thing," Nev said, clasping at his chest as if he was wounded. "What kind of a friend are you?"

"Well, it's the only reason I can think of as to why Hanley would be paying your father a visit," Elias said. "Though, of course, I know you would not ruin your father's reputation by doing such a thing."

"I wouldn't dare. Hanley scares the life out of me."

"Me too," Elias admitted. If Uriah Hanley was not there because of the bull, there was only one reason why he would have come to see Mr. Hill, and that reason was Elias.

He and Nev went about their chores through the afternoon, but Elias was distracted. He kept looking at the house. The longer Hanley stayed inside, the more nervous he got. It meant that Mr. Hill was listening to whatever he had to say.

"You don't have anything to worry about," Nev assured him as they lifted a log into place against the fence posts. "Dad already knows about your past."

"I know," Elias said as he hammered in a nail. He was still looking at the house and managed to hit his thumb instead of the nail. He cried out and immediately shook his hand, which made him drop his end of the log on his foot. "Can this day get any worse?" he said, exasperated at his own clumsiness.

"I know you're worried, but don't be. Dad's more than a

match for Hanley," Nev said as Elias picked the log back up and this time hammered the nail in fully.

"I know you think that, and your father is a good man," Elias said. "But I've been here before, with well-meaning men coming to tell my employer all about me and my past, and it never ends well for me."

"Dad won't listen to a load of gossip, and he certainly won't do anything he doesn't want to, not just to please a man like Hanley," Nev assured him. Elias raised an eyebrow quizzically. Mr. Hill had been more than ready to listen to the gossip about him in the past. Nev saw his look and grinned. "I know he wasn't keen on taking you on in the past, but he knows you now. He knows how hard you work and how honest you are."

"I am going to hope that you are right," Elias said, "but I reserve the right to be convinced that you aren't." Nev banged in the nail at his end, and they let the post go. It held. To be safe, they banged in a couple more nails each, then moved on to the next one.

The day passed slowly and the fence around the paddock was still not finished when Uriah Hanley left a little after four o'clock. Mr. Hill came out onto the deck and beckoned them forward. Elias had never felt more anxious in his life. It felt as though a hundred snakes were writhing in his belly as he waited for his employer to speak.

"Hanley felt that I should know that my new hand is a

thief," he said solemnly. "And that I'd be a fool to keep him on my land."

"And what did you tell him?"

"That I know all about your past and that it is my business who I employ," Mr. Hill said, shaking his head. "The gall of that man to come here and tell me how to run my ranch when his is failing so badly."

"How do you know that Fairview is failing?" Nev asked.

"Because no man sells his prize bull if it isn't," Elias said softly, shaking his head in disbelief that he'd not thought of it earlier.

"That's right," Mr. Hill agreed. "Surprised you boys hadn't worked that out by now."

"I didn't think," Nev admitted.

"Me neither," Elias said.

"And he's been selling land and is down to around half the head of cattle he used to run," Mr. Hill said with a wry smile. It was almost as if he found it amusing. "And he is not happy about it. Nope, he is not happy at all."

"So, he's angry and taking it out on anyone he can?" Elias said.

"No, he's angry and he's taking it out on you," Mr. Hill said, confirming Elias' fears. "When he found out he'd sold his bull to the man employing you, he got mad. He's out to get you, Elias, and though he's not doing well right now, his voice still holds sway in the ranching world."

"But I haven't done anything," Elias said. "What can he do to me?"

"That I don't know, but I am certain that he'll find some way to ruin you unless he sees me turn you out."

"You aren't going to," Nev exclaimed, aghast at the idea. "You can't. Elias is the best hand we've ever had. And he's my friend."

"I've no intention of turning Elias off our land. I'll not throw away the best worker this place has ever had to please that old coot," Mr. Hill said. "But I think he should be aware of what is happening around him. It should be up to him if he wants to stay and face whatever might come his way – knowing we will be on his side whatever Hanley throws his way – or if he wants to make a new start somewhere else."

"I want to stay," Elias said. He sighed heavily. "But I won't let him ruin you because of whatever it is he has against me."

"He's a bitter old man who thinks all criminals should hang," Mr. Hill said simply. "Even boys. He doesn't think you should have been given a second chance to live like everyone else. And I can assure you that he's committed more crimes in his life than you ever have. It never ceases to amaze me how often those with the worst crimes in their own past are the first to demand the harshest punishments for others."

"Uriah Hanley has broken the law?" Nev asked, his eyes wide with excitement. "In what ways?"

"He cheats," Mr. Hill said. "At cards, in business dealings. He's had men beaten so they'll do what he wants. There was a rumor before you were born that he'd even killed a man. And I know he thinks nothing of beating his wife. I know that's not a crime, but it should be. No man should ever beat on someone weaker than himself."

Nev gasped. "I knew he was a mean old coot, but I'd never have thought that of him."

"And he's losing everything that gives him his power and influence in the ranching community," Mr. Hill warned. "He's like a cornered rat. His voice may still hold some sway, but he can feel it all slipping away. He'll take anyone he can down with him, and he's decided that he'll start with Elias. As much as I want you to stay, lad, I must confess that I would advise you to get as far away from here as you can."

When the day was done, Elias made his way inside the bunkhouse. Mr. Hill had invited him to dine with the family, but he needed to think. If a man like Uriah Hanley wanted him gone, then somehow or another, Elias had no doubt, he would make that happen. And as Mr. Hill had said, Uriah didn't play fair. He'd not hesitate to create some fiction that would have Elias back in jail, or worse. He didn't want to leave. Camp Hill was his home and he had finally found people who accepted him as he was despite his past, but he couldn't help thinking that he had no other choice.

But where could he go? If Hanley was set on ruining his life, there was nowhere in New Mexico, Colorado, Utah, maybe not even Texas, that he could go. Hanley had dealings with men all across the South, as did Mr. Hill. He'd found finding work hard enough over the years, and the last thing he needed was Hanley stirring all that up again, making him unwanted wherever he might turn. He exhaled sharply and punched the wall by his bed. When he realized he'd grazed his knuckles badly, he laughed bitterly before pouring some water into the washing bowl and cleaning the wounds.

The thought of going to Miss Pauling crossed his mind as he bandaged his hand. Minnesota was certainly far enough away that he might be able to make a new start, but it was too soon to just turn up unannounced. He did not want to pressure her into anything. But perhaps he could move north and find work somewhere nearby and they could continue to write to each other until she was more comfortable with the idea of meeting him in person?

He couldn't sleep. All night, his mind was plagued with thoughts of what might happen if he stayed here and whether Hanley would be satisfied with just running him off. By dawn, he'd decided that he was going to leave. He did not want to cause the Hills any trouble, so he would go, but he was afraid that Hanley wouldn't be satisfied. The man wanted to see him hanging from a gallows, and Elias doubted anything less would please him.

There was a polite tap on the bunkhouse door. "Elias," Mr. Hill called. "There's a letter for you."

Elias opened the door. "Good morning, Sir," he said, taking the letter from Mr. Hill.

"You look like you didn't get a wink of sleep."

"I don't think I did," Elias admitted. "Hanley left me with a lot to think about."

"And have you made your decision?"

"I have. I'm going to go. I won't have you and Nev caught up in whatever grudge it is he has against me. I'll head north. There's ranches in Montana and Minnesota. I'll find work somewhere."

Mr. Hill nodded. "They'll be lucky to have you. We shall miss you. Make sure you write and let us know how you are getting along."

"And you'll tell me if you hear that Hanley is still out to get me?" Elias asked. "I don't want to spend my life looking over my shoulder."

"I will." The older man looked as though he was about to say something else but then thought better of it. "I'll let you get packed," he said before walking away.

Elias closed the door and sat down on his bed. He looked at the letter. It was from Miss Pauling. His heart lifted for just a moment, but then he cursed himself for a fool for not telling her about his past from the start. If he told her now, it might seem that he had been lying to her and that he was only telling her because he had been forced to leave because of it coming back to haunt him.

He opened the letter and began to read.

Dear Mr. Groves,

Thank you for your letter. I was delighted to receive it and to know that you cared enough for me to write it so I would not worry.

I want to write pages of things to you, but I can hardly bring myself to say anything. Writing simply is not enough. I want to talk with you in person. I know that this is very forward of me but, please, will you come to Iron Creek?

I know it is probably too soon. I know that we barely know one another. I know that you will have to travel the very length of the country to get here. But, please, come?

Life is too short to waste. I know that we cannot ever truly know if we suit unless we meet, so it is time. It is not too soon. It is not foolish.

Yours most hopefully

Marta Pauling

Had this arrived before Uriah Hanley's visit to the ranch, Elias would have gladly accepted her invitation. He had been waiting impatiently until enough time had passed before he proposed such a thing himself. Clearly, Miss Pauling had decided that she was not prepared to wait any longer than necessary, and that meant that she truly liked him. Just a day ago, that thought would have brought him so much joy.

But it was today, and everything had changed. Elias did not want Miss Pauling to think that he was only moving closer to her because he had nowhere else to go. How could he tell her what was happening to him and why? He barely understood it himself. Perhaps she would understand if he told her that he would come soon but that the time wasn't yet right? He could get himself settled somewhere and then go to her if she would wait.

And what if Uriah Hanley hounded him every step of the way? What if his leaving New Mexico was not enough to satisfy the bitter old man? Would he have to look over his shoulder every minute of every day for the rest of his life? Elias had to believe that leaving would be enough. Nev had promised him a letter of recommendation, and he hoped that Mr. Hill would give him one as well. He could take them and make a new start in the north. Perhaps Miss Pauling would forgive him for the delay in meeting her, but he couldn't help being afraid that she would turn away from him if she knew everything that he'd not yet told her.

CHAPTER 11

*A*ugust 20, 1890, Iron Creek, Minnesota

Every day for a week, Marta had raced to the postal office within five minutes of the mail train coming into the station, hoping that Mr. Groves had written and said that he was on his way. But there had been nothing. She couldn't help worrying that she had scared him away after all. But Emily and Richard kept telling her to be patient, that a letter would come soon. Or he would. Marta had tried to believe them, but with each passing day she was growing more and more certain that Mr. Groves would never come to Iron Creek.

The bell above the door jangled. "Gertie, can you get that?" she called from the kitchen. She was in the middle of kneading a large batch of bread dough. When there was no answer, Marta shook her head, suddenly remembering that she had sent Gertie to the General Store to get some more butter. She wiped down her hands and went into the shop. Katy Harding was peering hungrily at the cakes.

"What can I get for you today, Katy?" Marta asked.

"Oh, what I want is every single delicious cake you have, but what I need is two loaves of bread, a meat pie, and a fruitcake," Katy said with a smile. "I do not know how you work in a place like this and keep your figure. I'd eat everything in sight."

"You grow immune to it, a little," Marta said. She wrapped everything Katy had asked for and handed them to her. "I don't often see you in here."

"No, I mostly make all my own bread and cakes. It's a long way into town from our place, but Garrett has taken it upon himself to get us a new stove. He had time yesterday to rip the old one out, so I have no way of cooking anything until he puts the new one in."

"And when will that be?"

"I have no idea. He needs more help with the animals. I told him to just stick with sheep, but no, he had to take on a herd of cattle. Got himself a bargain, he said. But now, it's too much for him and the men he has, and he knows next to nothing about cattle. And then he decides to make changes in the house, as well. It's not so bad at the moment. The weather is fine and we can cook on a fire outside in the yard, but I'll be lucky if I'm not cooking our Christmas dinner over it if things don't change soon." With a rueful look, Katy paid Marta for the food and left the shop.

Marta couldn't help thinking about Garrett's need for a new hand, preferably one used to working with cows. It was almost as if God had meant for Mr. Groves to come to Iron Creek right then. There would be a letter from him soon. There had to be. It was too much of a coincidence for him not to write and say he was on his way.

Gertie bundled into the shop, making the door clang more loudly than usual. "I got the butter, and they had some vanilla. I know you said we were a little low, so I thought it might be an idea to have some in case your order is delayed."

"Well done," Marta said, taking the basket from her young apprentice.

"And Mr. Wilson caught me and gave me this." Gertie handed Marta a letter. "Is it from your young man, do you think?"

"It is," Marta said happily, looking at the sloping scrawl on the envelope. "Now, get back to work, there's dough that needs kneading back there."

Gertie giggled but did as she was told. Marta ripped open the letter.

Dear Miss Pauling,

Thank you for your invitation to come and meet with you in your hometown. One day, I shall most certainly do so. I have decided to move further north so I might be closer to you, and for reasons I shall explain in greater detail as soon as I can do so in person. I ask you to be patient with me, though, as I will need to find myself a position before I can do that. I won't come to you a destitute vagabond.

I am not sure how long it will take, but I have enclosed a list of the places I shall be stopping at on my way. You can write to me there. And if you hear of any ranches that need a hardworking hand, please do let me know.

Yours adventurously

Elias Groves

It was a short letter, but it told Marta everything she wanted to hear. He was on his way, even if it was not directly to Iron Creek. He cared about her enough to move all this way, to take a chance that their relationship might work. And she did know of a position. She glanced at the first few addresses on the list and hurried out of the shop and across the road to the postal office.

"I need to send this message," she said to Hank Wilson as she scribbled a few words and the Hardings' address on one of the telegram forms he kept on the counter, "to these three places."

"Not sure which one he'll be at?" Mr. Wilson said with a smile. "Well, let's hope we catch him at one of them. I'll send them immediately."

Marta paid for the telegrams and went back to the bakery. She would have a nervous wait, but she couldn't help feeling that fate had stepped in and was smoothing the path for her and Mr. Groves. She prayed he would not think that it was too soon to be so close by and that he would see the benefit of them being able to see each other every day if they wished to. And she prayed that Garrett would like him as much as she did.

When she closed up, she decided to take a trip up the mountain to speak with Garrett in person. It seemed only right to warn him that a complete stranger might be getting in touch with him about a position on his farm. It was a long walk, but she knew she'd have enough time to get back before it got dark. It would mean she'd be later to bed than she preferred to be, but that couldn't be helped. It wasn't as if she was sleeping that much recently anyway.

When she reached the sprawling farmhouse, Marta couldn't help smiling at the scene in front of her. Katy and her children were sitting around the fire, talking and laughing as they prepared a meal. Garrett's adoptive mother, Zaaga, was showing the smaller ones how to toast bread over the flames using a long, green stick.

Marta had heard about Zaaga but had not yet met her. She was dark haired and dark skinned with a wise-looking face that had probably been very beautiful in her youth. She was still handsome, and she had sparkling eyes that seemed to see right through you. Marta longed to ask her a hundred questions about her life with the Ojibwe and how strange it must be to move between her world there and Garrett's in Iron Creek, but she just stared, even though she knew she was being rude. Thankfully, it seemed that Zaaga was too immersed in what she was doing to notice.

"Marta!" Katy said, suddenly noticing her. "Whatever are you doing up here?"

"I came to see Garrett, about what we talked about this morning."

"My stove?" Katy said, looking confused.

"No, that he needs some help with the cattle," Marta said with a grin.

"You know someone?" she asked eagerly.

"I think I might."

"Oh, that would be the best news," Katy said. She glanced at Zaaga, who nodded her agreement.

"Garrett is too stubborn. He waits until it is too late to do anything. He always has," Zaaga said lovingly.

"Even marrying me," Katy said with a smile. "But he gets there in the end. He's in the barn, I think. Do you want me to fetch him for you?"

"No, I can go. You all look like you're having fun."

"We won't be if we have to do it for much longer," Katy joked.

The barn was cool and dark. Marta could hear voices at the very back, so she made her way toward them. She heard a sheep bleating loudly, as if it was in pain. A lantern was hanging up on the wall above a stall. Thick straw lay on the ground, and there was a tired-looking sheep on top of it. Two men were crouching beside her. Marta recognized Garrett

Harding but not the Ojibwe man next to him. Whoever he was, he was tall and handsome, and he was being very gentle with the distressed animal.

"Come on, Bessie, I know it's tough," Garrett said. "But the sooner you push your little one out, the sooner this is all over."

"I'll have to slice her belly if she doesn't deliver soon, or we'll lose them both," the other man said sadly. "She's getting too weak."

Garrett stood up, shaking his head. "Do it," he said. Marta could hear the regret in his tone. "I'll get everything you need."

He climbed over the gate of the pen and only then noticed Marta. "This isn't a great time," he said as he made his way to a trunk pushed against the back wall of the barn.

"I can see that, but I think I may have good news for you."

"I could use some of that. Bessie is one of the first ewes I birthed when I took on this place, so losing her feels like the worst thing that could happen."

"I know a cowboy. He's coming north, and he needs a job," Marta said, staring as Garrett lifted the lid of the trunk and pulled out a very sharp-looking knife.

"Then get him to come and see me as soon as he can," Garrett said. "I'll welcome him with open arms."

"As simple as that?" she asked incredulously.

"As simple as that," Garrett agreed. "I'm not in a position to be choosy. Not many men who know anything about cattle are knocking on my door." Marta nodded, and watched as he went back to Bessie and handed the knife to his companion. "Dibikad, be careful with them both," he said cautiously.

But as he said it, Bessie gave an almighty heave and Garrett's face lit up. Dibikad eased his hand gently inside the ewe. "I can feel the lamb," Dibikad said excitedly as he pulled the little one out. It landed on the floor in a puddle of fluid. Garrett moved the lamb to its mother's head so she could lick away the birthing sac that clung to its tiny body. They all watched in silence as they waited for Bessie to do so, and they all sighed when she started to do it.

"Well, perhaps my luck is changing," Garrett said, grinning first at Dibikad, then at Marta. "Your cowboy, will he be here soon?"

"I certainly hope so," Marta said before leaving the barn and making her way back to the fire.

"How is Bessie?" Katy asked.

"She is doing well now, I think," Marta said, still a little overwhelmed by what she'd just seen. "The lamb is alive and was trying to get on its feet as I left."

"That is good news. Garrett will be happy."

"I think Dibikad, I hope I am saying that correctly." Marta paused and looked at Zaaga, who nodded that she was. "I think that Dibikad probably is too. They were getting ready to cut the lamb out."

"It would have broken Garrett's heart to lose Bessie. She was kept aside when we put the ram in with the ewes for the spring lambing. Garrett didn't want her to have to go through it all again. Clearly, she had other ideas because she managed to get out of the pen and found him anyway." Katy grinned at the thought of her sheep getting out to find her man. "That's why she's having her lamb so late."

"Love finds a way, I suppose," Marta said with a smile.

"It does," Zaaga said. "And I am glad. If Dibikad had been the one to take Bessie's life, their friendship would have been over, forever this time. I have been fearful of that for some time."

"They seemed as close as brothers in the barn," Marta said, puzzled by what Zaaga had just said.

"Dibikad took Garrett's first wife as a lover. It broke their bond, but they've worked hard to put that in the past, where it belongs," Katy explained. "Zaaga was right to be worried, but this will only strengthen their friendship."

Marta was happy for the two men but couldn't help feeling she had just learned far more about the Hardings' personal matters than she had any right to know. "I should go now, or I'll not get home before dark," she said politely.

"Thank you," Katy said. "I do hope your cowboy gets here soon. Garrett needs him."

"I hope I will hear from him soon. I sent a telegram this afternoon. I'll let you know as soon as I hear from him," she promised.

As she walked down the road to town, a nagging doubt kept circling her head. She prayed that she had not got the Hardings' hopes up too soon. What if Mr. Groves did not want to come to Iron Creek straight away? What if he thought that it was too soon for him to live so close by? What if they did not get along and were forced to see each other every day because she had dragged him here? There was so much that could go wrong, and she could not help feeling scared that she had done the wrong thing by both her friends and Mr. Groves.

CHAPTER 12

August 21, 1890, Kansas City, Missouri

Elias was already fed up with traveling. He didn't have much money, even though Mr. Hill had been kind enough to give him a generous bonus on top of his wages when he'd left. In order to get to where he wanted to go, he needed to take the slowest and cheapest options available to him – wagon trains, riding alone, and on the few slow trains that had a cattle car so Jet could travel with him. Jet was too good a horse to leave behind, though Mr. Hill had offered a fine price for him.

As the miles passed endlessly, he thought about what to do and how he could explain things to Miss Pauling when they met. He still had not found a way to do so that did not have her hating him once he had told her everything she needed to know. He simply could not bear that thought, so he worked hard to convince himself that there was no need for Miss Pauling to know everything. After all, he truly was leaving his past behind him this time. There was no reason for him to let it taint his future with Miss Pauling. The only thing that mattered was who he was now, and he had not lied to her about that. She knew Elias Groves better than anyone alive, even though they had shared barely a handful of letters. He had told her about himself in a way he had never done with anyone before. Surely that was not lying to her?

There was a nagging doubt in the back of his mind, but he had almost convinced himself that it was for the best to start his life afresh by the time the train reached Kansas City. He had worked hard his entire life, harder than those who hadn't had so much to prove to gain their place on a ranch. He was a good man. He deserved a little of the happiness that others took for granted. For once in his life, he was going to do what was best for him rather than try to do what was right. Miss Pauling was what was best for him, and he was certain that she would not want him if she knew the whole truth, so it was best that she never found it.

The boarding house that Mr. Hill had suggested to him was clean, but that was about all that could be said for it. The bed was the lumpiest thing that he'd ever slept on, and the food was barely edible. Luckily, he was only there for two nights, so he could bear it. On the plus side, there had been a surprise waiting for him upon his arrival – a telegram from Miss Pauling, telling him that there was a position for him in Iron Creek itself. His happiness at the news had lasted for at least an hour before he remembered all the things he had not yet told her. He wondered if he should even write to Mr. Harding under the circumstances.

After a sleepless night, partly because of his racing thoughts and mostly because of the sheer discomfort of the bed, he decided he would write to her straight away. He needed work and this was a position that would suit him well. He was not able to be choosy under the circumstances. He decided to send a telegram, as Miss Pauling had done. It would get to its destination more quickly than the mail, even if it was much more expensive.

Kansas City was bigger than any place he'd ever been. And it was busy. People, dogs, horses, carriages, wagons... everywhere he looked, someone was doing something. He had to keep alert to ensure he did not get run down as he crossed the street. He got lost a couple of times on his way to the telegram office, but the clerk there was very helpful. He left feeling sure that both Miss Pauling and Mr. Harding would receive the news with the very least delay.

He had an entire day before his next train, so he wandered aimlessly around the city. He found it fascinating. The speed of the place was quite remarkable; everyone seemed in a big hurry. He was the only person walking with no purpose, and he stood out in his denim pants and plaid shirt. All the men were either dressed in black or gray suits or grubby work clothes. It wasn't a place he'd want to live, but it was definitely interesting.

His best find was a small theater that had a matinee playing. He paid a few pennies for a ticket and went inside. He remembered Miss Pauling saying how much she enjoyed the theater in Iron Creek as he settled himself in the seat. The play was a little dull – a man and a woman fought among themselves for most of it before finally deciding that they were in love – but the experience was a delight. The darkness, the thick velvet curtains that hid the stage, the face paint that the actors wore to accentuate their features, and the chance to leave the real world behind him, even if only for a couple of hours, somehow made it magical.

Back at the boarding house, he sat down and wrote a letter to Miss Pauling. He wanted to tell her about going to the theater and the cattle market. He'd barely had time to think, and it was nice to tell her all about the things that had happened. He didn't tell her about Uriah Hanley's visit to Camp Hill. He had decided, after much deliberation, that she did not need to know about any of that. It felt strange not to tell her. A part of him desperately wanted to confide in her, but he could not. Surely his past would not catch up to him so very far away, so there was no reason to tell her something that would only hurt them both?

He sealed the letter and wondered if it was worth sending it. Guessing it might reach her before he did, especially as the mail traveled on trains much faster than those he was taking, he decided to ask the lady who ran the boarding house to mail it for him in the morning. For a moment, he sat just thinking about what it would be like to meet Miss Pauling. He was looking forward to it very much, even though he knew he was being a coward by not telling her everything.

But that blessed day was still weeks away. With a heavy sigh, Elias pulled the blankets off the bed onto the floor. He was convinced that it would be more comfortable on the hard floorboards than it had been on the lumpy bed the night before. He undressed and lay down, wondering what the bunkhouse at Garrett Harding's place would be like. Some places had big bunkhouses, though it was rare they were filled with men. They were only ever filled on farms around harvest time, and on a ranch before and after a big drive across state lines. Most permanent ranch hands lived alone. He'd liked the one at Camp Hill. It had been warm and comfortable. As he closed his eyes and prayed for sleep, he hoped for something similar in Iron Creek.

AUGUST 22, 1890, Iron Creek, Minnesota

The bell above the shop door jangled loudly. Marta brushed off her hands and made her way along the corridor. Hank Wilson was standing in front of the counter looking red-faced and out of breath.

"Miss Pauling, he replied," he said between gasps, holding out a telegram to her.

"He did?" Marta asked, taking it from him. "Do you need to sit down? A glass of water, perhaps?"

"Not at all. I must take another telegram from him to Mr. Harding."

"Might I suggest that you don't run all the way up the mountain," Marta teased him gently.

He smiled at her. "I shall take the gig. But I knew you would want to see yours straight away."

"You were right, I do. Thank you, Mr. Wilson." Knowing he would not leave until she opened it and saw what was inside, she opened it and read it out loud.

On my way. Position sounds ideal. There in three weeks.
Elias Groves

He hadn't wasted any words. Mr. Wilson beamed at her. "Are you happy?"

"I am," she said. "Now, you can go and tell all of Iron Creek that I have a gentleman friend coming to visit."

"I would never," he protested, his face turning red again.

"You would, and I don't mind," Marta said happily. "I just ask you to wait until tomorrow so I can tell Emily before she finds out my news from someone else."

"I swear," he vowed solemnly.

The rest of Marta's day passed painfully slowly. She wanted to close the shop early and run straight to Emily's house to tell her everything, but Gertie was off sick, so she was alone, and Fridays were often busy as people bought everything they needed for the weekend. When the clock finally ticked past three o'clock, she sighed with relief. She turned the sign on the door to *closed*, locked the door, and pulled down the blinds. After cleaning everything she hadn't already cleaned, she let herself out of the back door and ran to Emily's.

She arrived at the Balls' house as red-faced and breathless as Mr. Wilson had been at the bakery earlier and pounded on the door. Mrs. Ball answered it with a warm smile.

"Well, good day to you, Marta, dear," she said. "Are you staying for dinner with us? Mayor Winston is, so you'd be eating alone if you went home again, I'm afraid."

"I would love to," Marta said. She always enjoyed the big family meals around the Balls' vast kitchen table. "Thank you for inviting me."

"Emily and her father are in the back garden. He's teaching her how to tie in her beans. They've grown quite rampant."

Marta went through the house and into the back garden. She found Mayor Winston and Emily at the very end of the garden, hidden behind the beans. Mrs. Ball had described them well – they had grown very tall and straggly and seemed to be sending out tendrils everywhere.

"This is a nice surprise," Emily said, beaming at Marta. "We don't often see you on a Friday."

"She usually just goes straight to bed when she gets in," Mayor Winston said. "It is a long week when you are up so early every day."

"It is," Marta agreed. "But I have news that I have to share with you."

"You do?" Emily asked. She handed the string to her father and came out from the beans, then tucked an arm through Marta's and walked her up the garden path. "What is it?"

"He's coming," Marta said excitedly.

"Who's coming?"

"Mr. Groves, you ninny."

"Oh," Emily said, her eyes wide. "Are we happy or nervous, or petrified?"

"A little of all three, I think," Marta admitted.

"And when does he arrive?"

"He said in three weeks."

"That isn't very long. Goodness. Where will he stay when he gets here? What will he do?"

It was typical of Emily to think of the practicalities. Marta had been too excited to even consider them. He would need somewhere to stay, even if it was only temporary. There was no point assuming that he would definitely get the position with Garrett just because he was a cowboy and Garrett needed one. And she wasn't sure if Garrett had anywhere suitable for Mr. Groves to live even if he did.

"I shall ask Nelly," she said, thinking of the most

obvious solution. "I doubt he'll be able to afford the hotel, but Nelly doesn't charge her lodgers much, I don't think."

"I can ask her tomorrow. I will be in the clinic with her. I'm sure she'd be happy to put him up. I don't think she has anyone staying with her at the moment, and I think she's a bit lonely because of it."

"That is very good news," Marta said. "And I'm hoping that Garrett will give him a job. He said he would talk with him, and he desperately needs someone who knows anything about cattle, and Mr. Groves is a cowboy."

"Then we shall hope that they get along and Garrett does indeed take him on," Emily said firmly. "And what about you? Are you sure this is what you want?"

"Oh, Emily, I do," Marta said. "From his very first letter, he has fascinated me. I am so looking forward to meeting him. I do so hope he will like me."

"He will love you unless he is an utter fool. You are the very best person I know."

"Thank you. You are the very best friend a girl could ask for. You donated your father to me and brought me a whole new life, and you are now calming my nerves as I prepare to meet the man I hope will love me as much as Richard loves you. I do not know what I would do without you."

"You'd be a mess, as I would be without you," Emily said with a grin. "Now, come inside and see the flowers that Mayor Winston brought Aunt Mary."

CHAPTER 13

September 17, 1890, Iron Creek, Minnesota

Marta paced up and down on the platform, impatient for the train to arrive. She'd been there to meet every train coming in from Duluth every day that week. Mr. Groves hadn't said which day he expected to arrive, just that it would take three weeks, and she'd not wanted to risk him arriving with nobody there to greet him. But it had been three weeks from when he'd sent the telegram and there was still no sign of him. At the beginning of the week, she'd hoped he would be early, then she'd accepted he'd take the full three weeks, and now she was beginning to suspect he wasn't coming at all.

She heard the whistle of the train and saw a plume of smoke and steam in the distance. As she waited for the locomotive to reach the station, she bit her nails nervously. He had to come today. She would stop coming to meet him if he did not. He could come and find her. She'd wasted enough time on him, and though Gertie was perfectly capable of running the bakery in her absence, she couldn't keep expecting the girl to do so alone.

The train pulled to a halt, its brakes screeching loudly, and a fog of smoke and steam filled the platform. Marta waited for it to clear, then peered up and down the row of carriages, wondering if he would step down from one of the opening doors this time. A young man helped an elderly gentleman down. He was followed by a mother with three children and a small, yappy dog. Last of all, a white-haired lady in a fabulously feathered hat descended. All of them were met with hugs and kisses from loved ones. There was nobody else.

Her heart sinking, Marta turned to leave the station. She was halfway through the ticket office when Gerald Singer, the new station guard, caught up with her. "Miss Pauling, there's a gentleman here for you," he said, beaming at her, his ruddy cheeks flushed even more than normal from the exertion he'd made.

"Are you sure? I didn't see anyone get down from the train?"

"He was in the animal cart, at the rear," Gerald explained. "His horse was sick. He threw the cart door open while the train was still moving and yelled at me to see if you were here. He didn't want to miss you."

Marta turned back to the platform, and sure enough, a tall young man dressed in a plaid shirt and denim pants was leading a chestnut horse toward her. His Stetson sat at a jaunty angle on his head, hiding his face a little from her view, but he swept it off his head and gave her a nodding bow as soon as he saw her.

"Miss Pauling, I am so glad Mr. Singer found you," he said with a smile that made Marta's heart pound far too fast.

"Mr. Groves? It is really you," she said, a little flustered at the sight of his chiseled features and tanned skin. His eyes were a vivid green, and they made her feel more than a little peculiar as they steadily gazed at her. How could he be so calm? She was a nervous wreck.

"It is, and this fella here is Jet," he said, nodding toward his horse. "Jet doesn't much like traveling by rail, so we're both glad to be here." His voice was deep and rich, and he had a Southern drawl that made every word he said seem somehow strange and so much more enthralling than anyone else might have made them sound. She had liked him immensely from his letters, but he was overwhelming in the flesh.

To try to gather herself a little, she stepped forward and stroked Jet's nose. "He's a fine animal," she said.

"He is, though he's been nothing but trouble the whole way."

"I hope that he'll feel more like himself again once he settles on solid ground once more."

"I do, too," Mr. Groves said. "Otherwise, I may come to regret not taking Mr. Hill's offer to buy him from me when I left."

"I've arranged for you to stay with Mrs. Graham. She's just a short walk from here. The public stable is on the way, and I'm sure Alec will be able to find a stall for Jet."

"That's mighty kind of you, but I'll be staying up at the Hardings' place," Mr. Groves said. "Mr. Harding said he'd fix me up a spot in his bunkhouse, with his other workers. If you've gone to any expense, you must let me know and I'll reimburse you for it."

"No, none," Marta said, feeling a little sad that he wouldn't be in town, at least for a little while. The Hardings' place was a way up the mountain, and he might not find many reasons to come into Iron Creek once he got himself settled and busy with his work there.

"But I'd very much like to go walking with you, if I may?" he asked eagerly.

"It would have to be on Sunday, after church," Marta said a little nervously. "As a baker, my waking hours are a little peculiar."

"I can imagine," he said, smiling. "I am always amazed that everything in a bakery is fresh and perfect so early in the morning."

"It means starting work very early and going to bed before most people have even had their supper."

They walked out of the station and onto Main Street.

Mr. Groves nodded a little as he looked up and down the street. "It's nice," he said. "Not at all what I was expecting."

"What were you expecting?" she asked as they walked slowly along the busy street, full of shops and other businesses.

"I don't really know. A small place with not much going on, I suppose. Perhaps a little like those streets you read in the newspapers, where brave, pioneering souls have made their homes despite the hardships."

Marta laughed. "You know, I rather imagined that being the kind of place you've just come from."

"To be honest, it was much like that," Mr. Groves admitted with a chuckle. "This is altogether more civilized."

They had reached the bakery, and as always a delicious smell was wafting out onto the street. "Something smells incredible," he said, sniffing eagerly, his eyes lighting up like a small boy's.

"Come inside. I'm sure I can find you something tasty to try. You've probably not eaten anything good in days, stuck on that train."

"Weeks," he said.

Gertie hurried into the shop from the kitchen at the sound of the bell, then saw it was Marta. She stopped and stared at Mr. Groves, her mouth open wide like a fish's.

"Gertie, I'm sure you have something to do in the kitchen," Marta said, moving behind the counter and prodding her apprentice a little. Gertie gulped, looked at Marta, back at Mr. Groves, then turned and fled into the kitchen.

Marta couldn't blame the girl for her reaction. Mr. Groves was larger than life, especially now he was inside a normal-sized building. He was the tallest man Marta had ever met. She barely reached his chin, and she was a very tall woman. It was refreshing that he was taller than her, but also a little daunting. And he was too handsome, yet she didn't get the impression that he thought much of his looks. He didn't seem to care that heads turned as he walked along the street, or that girls stared at him the way Gertie had.

He was more interested in the food. As he took in the array of breads, pies, and pastries on the counter, he shook his head again. A loud grumble from his belly told Marta just how hungry he was, so she took a meat pie and a slice of sponge cake, put them on plates, and handed him a knife and fork. When she had done that, she fetched a chair from the kitchen office and placed it in front of the counter. As she did so, she thought about adding a few tables and chairs so customers could sit in the shop and enjoy something to eat and a cup of tea or coffee.

"Eat," she said.

He ate hungrily, murmuring words of praise every few mouthfuls. When he was finished, he pushed the plates away and beamed at her. "That was the best food I have ever eaten."

"Thank you," Marta said, blushing at his compliment.

"But I suppose I should be on my way. Mr. Harding said his place is a way up the mountain, and I'd rather get there before it gets dark and I get lost up there."

Marta's heart sank. She didn't want him to leave, – though it made sense for him to get to his destination in the remaining daylight. "If you're sure you must go straight away," she said.

"I'd rather stay and talk to you all night, but I'm sure you have work to do. If you could point me in the direction I need to go, I would be very grateful."

Reluctantly, she did so, even writing him out a little map with landmarks to look out for so he'd not get lost. The farmhouse wasn't hard to find as long as you took the right track up the mountain. She watched him make his way along Main Street and didn't go inside until she saw his distant figure turn up the right track. He didn't turn back, not even once. But why should he? He had other things on his mind than her, not getting lost being the most important.

She went back inside, and Gertie burst into the shop. "Who was that? Was that your gentleman friend? Is he coming back again later? Does he like you? Do you like him? Did you see his hair? His eyes?"

"Gertie, precisely which one of those questions would you like me to answer first?" Marta said with an indulgent smile at the young girl's excitement.

"I didn't think it was possible for anyone to be that handsome," Gertie said with a sigh.

"I'm not sure that I did, either," Marta admitted.

"Will you be seeing him soon? Will he be calling on you? A man like that could call on me anytime he likes."

"We will go walking together after church on Sunday," Marta said.

"You are so lucky," Gertie said, peering out the shop window as if she might catch a glimpse of Mr. Groves once more.

"I don't know about that, not yet," Marta said. "He might not like me at all."

"Everybody likes you, Marta. And no man would ever turn down having you cook for him for the rest of his life."

"They do say that the way to a man's heart is through his stomach. If that is true, then I have a hope," Marta said with a grin.

"More than a hope," Gertie said, giggling. "There's nobody in town that can cook like you."

"Back to work, you minx," Marta chided gently. "We have much to do before we close today."

The two of them prepared the dough for the next day's bread and left it to prove overnight in large bowls covered with cloth, served customers, and cleaned the place from top to bottom before closing up. Marta did not feel ready to go home. She needed to speak to Emily, but Emily would be at work. If she was lucky, though, the clinic would be quiet and Emily would have a few minutes to talk.

When she arrived, the waiting room was empty. She

suddenly remembered that she needed to tell Nelly Graham that the room would not be needed after all and hoped Nelly wouldn't be too disappointed. The older woman had seemed rather excited about having a boarder. Marta took a seat and waited for someone to respond to the sound of the door opening. It didn't take long for Emily to emerge, her apron stained with blood.

"Oh my, what happened?" Marta asked, jumping to her feet.

Emily laughed. "Nothing much. The Jellicoe twins have been fighting again, and they both came in with terrible nosebleeds. You'd think they'd have a little less energy for fighting now they both have jobs."

"Those two are devils," Marta said. "I don't know how such calm, sweet people as Hector and Mary could have produced such hellions."

"They're good boys, really," Emily said. "They work hard. They're just terrors when they're together. Now, what can I do for you?"

"He's here," Marta said.

"He is?" Emily looked around as if he might be in the room with them.

"Not literally *here*," Marta said with a nervous giggle. "Here in Iron Creek."

"And?"

"He's far too handsome, and tall. He's very tall."

"Well, that's good, because you are too."

"He's too handsome for the likes of me," Marta said.

"Nonsense. You're beautiful, especially when you aren't covered in flour," Emily assured her. "But what is he actually like? Did you get a sense of his personality?"

"He seems nice, polite," Marta said thoughtfully. "I'm to go walking with him on Sunday after church."

"Then I shall come to Dad's early and help you to fix your hair and calm you down."

"You are the best of friends," Marta said.

"You have been there for me through similar ups and downs, Marta. It is the very least I can do for you."

CHAPTER 14

Sunday, September 21, 1890, Iron Creek, Minnesota

Elias had enjoyed his first few days in Iron Creek. Garrett was a good man and a fair employer. He'd been happy with the letters of recommendation that Mr. Hill and Nev had written and had put Elias straight to work the morning after his arrival. He had even given Elias his own area of the bunkhouse, with a comfortable bed, a washstand, a comfortable armchair, and a small cupboard where he could keep his things. The other hands were friendly and pleased to see him. In truth, they couldn't wait to not have to worry about the cattle so they could just deal with the sheep they understood.

But every night, he'd lain awake with thoughts of Miss Pauling. She was a fine-looking woman. She was taller than many men, but he didn't mind that – or that she ran her own bakery – and he knew many men would have felt threatened by both those things. After eating that pie and the slice of cake, he knew that there was no way anyone should stop her from doing her job. She was a genius, and he couldn't wait to be fed by her again. He was sure that her hair was blonde, but it had been pinned up under a hat, so he wasn't entirely sure, and she had the biggest, bluest eyes that he had ever seen. He couldn't wait to see her again, so he hurried through his chores before washing thoroughly and pulling on his Sunday finest.

Mrs. Harding was herding the children into a wagon as he left the bunkhouse. "Do you want a lift to church?" she asked him.

"I'd not say no," he said, helping her to lift the little ones up.

"Garrett isn't coming today, so it'd be fine with me if you'd like to drive," she said as she pulled herself up onto the bench at the front of the wagon. He climbed up and took the reins, then clicked to the horse in the shafts to walk on.

"How are you finding us so far?" Mrs. Harding asked.

"I like it here," he said. "I'm grateful to Garrett for giving a stranger a job."

"He's a good judge of character. He knows who he likes."

"Well, I hope I don't let him down, Mrs. Harding."

"Katy. Call me Katy. There are no formalities around here," she said with a smile.

"I'll do that," he said.

For a moment, he wished he could confide in her and Garrett, but he had already grown to like these people very much and did not want to find himself on the road again, searching for work. Instead, he decided to ask about Marta. "Do you know Miss Pauling, at all?"

"A little," Katy said. "She's not been here all that long, but she won us all over with the things she bakes. The man she's in business with, Wes Baker, well, we all thought that he was the finest baker we'd ever known until she came here."

"Where's he now? I didn't see him at the bakery the other day."

"He runs their second store, in Grand Marais. I'd not be surprised to see them open stores all across the state. They're both very clever, very passionate about what they do, and everyone loves their food."

"So, you think she'd choose her work over becoming a wife and mother?" he asked, suddenly a little anxious that Miss Pauling might not want a more traditional life.

"I honestly don't know her well enough to say," Katy said. "But given that many women in town seem to manage both, why should she have to choose?"

"You make a good point," Elias said with a smile.

Katy pointed out all manner of birds and plants as they

made their way down the track to Iron Creek. Elias wasn't entirely sure if she was doing so for him or for the children in the back, but everyone seemed to be enjoying the lessons. It was a bright if rather chilly day, and Katy warned him that it wouldn't be long before frost and snow came to the higher ground.

"We have long winters here, and they are bitterly cold," she told him. "It's a harsh land at times, but on a day like today, you forget that and just enjoy its beauty."

"It is lovely. So green and full of life. It may have been warmer where I come from, but it's definitely prettier here."

"I'm glad you like it. Garrett's tied to the land here. Whether that's because of his growing up among the Ojibwe or just because he loves it, I don't know. I can't ever imagine leaving now, either. I don't think there's many people who've come here that do. Wes and his wife are the only people I can think of that ever have."

"I've only been here a few days, and I can't imagine being anywhere else," Elias admitted, and he was amazed to realize that he meant it. He'd never felt at home anywhere before. He'd known that he would be likely to be moving on from everywhere he'd gone. This was the only place he'd ever been where he didn't feel that way. He was sure he could build a life here, a good life, and he prayed that Miss Pauling would want to be a part of that life. He'd enjoyed her letters, but meeting her had only made him feel more strongly for her.

"Catholic or Protestant?" Katy said as they reached town.

"Sorry?" he asked, a little confused.

"Which are you?"

"Not really anything," he admitted. "Which church does Miss Pauling go to?"

"Catholic," Katy said. "Keep driving to the end of town. We want the church and not the chapel at this end."

It was hard to find anywhere to tie up the wagon in front of either place of worship. People in Iron Creek obviously took their churchgoing very seriously. Elias helped Katy get the children out of the back of the wagon and followed her inside the church. It smelled of incense inside, and the pews were almost all full. She pointed toward one near the front, and he led the way. Once they were all settled in their seats, he looked around. In the very front pew sat the mayor, flanked by two young women, a man about the same age as Elias, and an older woman.

One of the young women turned and looked anxiously around the church. Elias smiled when he realized it was Miss Pauling. Her hair fell down over her shoulders in a golden wave, and she was wearing a very pretty dress with a floral pattern. She smiled awkwardly and waved at him. He waved back. "How are you?" she mouthed.

"I'm well," he mouthed back. "Do you still wish to go walking?"

"I do."

Suddenly the congregation all stood up as two altar boys, one carrying a censer and wafting incense as he walked and the other carrying a crucifix, made their way up the aisle. They were followed by the priest. He had a kind face, and he delivered the service and his sermon with humor and humility. Despite his faith, Elias hadn't attended church much. After the troubles in his life, he'd not really felt that there was anyone looking out for him, after all, Uriah Hanley and Mr. Greenwood had both been regular churchgoers. It hadn't stopped them from being cruel people. But the way Father Paul spoke made him feel that perhaps there was more to religion than just appearing pious.

When the service drew to a close, Elias began to feel nervous. He'd never taken a girl walking before. He so wanted to make a good impression on Miss Pauling, but he feared that he might say something he might regret and make her hate him forever. So, as everyone began to file out of the church, he stayed behind for a moment, staring up at the crucifix that the altar boy had set in a bracket at the back of the altar. "Dear Lord, if you are up there, help me get this right," he said softly, then he crossed himself as he had seen everyone else do.

Father Paul was standing at the doorway, greeting everyone warmly as they departed. "You must be Elias Groves," he said, holding out a hand for Elias to shake. Elias took it and was surprised when the priest placed his other hand on top. "It is good to have a new member of our community."

"You know my name?"

"I make it my business to know," Father Paul said with a smile. "And I am glad that you chose to worship with us this fine Sunday."

"Thank you. I haven't been to church much recently," Elias said, surprised to find himself confessing such a thing. There was something very open about the priest, and he felt like he could tell him anything.

"Well, if you would like further guidance, my door is always open."

"Thank you. I may stop by someday."

"I hope you do," Father Paul said. He looked deep into Elias' eyes as if he were searching his soul. Elias prayed that the perceptive man could not see his demons and said goodbye.

Many people were still milling around and chatting in the fall sunshine. Elias saw Miss Pauling standing with the young woman who had been in the pew with her. He made his way over to them. "Good day to you," he said politely, removing his Stetson and giving them a nodding bow.

"And to you," Miss Pauling said. "This is my friend, Emily Ball. Emily, this is Mr. Elias Groves."

"A pleasure," Elias said.

"For me, too," Mrs. Ball said. She looked around briefly, her eyes alighting on the man who had sat beside her in church. She beckoned him over from the group he was talking to. "This is my husband, Richard. Richard, this is Elias Groves."

The two men shook hands firmly. "You must come for lunch," Richard said.

"Thank you," Elias said. "That is most generous of you."

"No trouble. Half the town seems to eat with us most Sundays."

"That is hardly true, Richard," Mrs. Ball said reproachfully. "It is only my father and Marta who join us."

"And Nelly and Mrs. Cable, and whoever else is alone for even a moment," Richard teased his wife.

She frowned at him, then turned back to Elias with a warm smile. "Marta can bring you with her after your walk." With that, she dragged her husband away, leaving Elias alone with Miss Pauling.

Marta smiled at him a little shyly. "Please forgive them. They are in the first throes of love and assume that everyone else must be in need of what they have."

Elias smiled at her. Her nerves were serving to actually make him feel calmer. "I wouldn't be opposed to that," he said softly.

"I doubt I would be against it, either," she admitted.

"So, where shall we take our walk?" he asked. "We seem to have been blessed with rather wonderful weather for it."

"Indeed," she said. "Would you like to see the creek that

the town is named for? Or perhaps take a walk in the woods? There are all manner of animals to see there."

"The creek would be nice. I've seen enough animals this week, I think," he said with a wry smile.

"That sounds intriguing?" she said, boldly tucking an arm through his.

"Garrett's herd is a little unruly. They've been run by men who have no idea how to do so for too long, so they are badly behaved and I'm having to train them all over again."

"That sounds like hard work," she said as she led them toward a narrow path along the side of the church wall.

"It is, but it'll be worth it. Garrett wants to drive them up to Minneapolis for the markets there in the spring. I just hope we've got time."

They walked in silence for a few hundred yards. The path took them through a quiet woodland that smelled of moss and pine and gently rotting wood. Elias wondered if Miss Pauling simply had nothing to say and he should try to fill the silence. He'd never met a girl who didn't talk at him the entire time he was with them before. It felt strange, but when he looked at her face, he saw that she was avidly searching the woodland floor for footprints.

"Do you hope to see something in particular?" he whispered.

"Emily told me that she saw a stag here once. I keep hoping that I will one day, too," she said with a smile.

"Now I do, as well," he said, grinning.

"How are you finding Iron Creek," she asked as they left the woods and came out on the banks of the creek.

"I don't know much about the town yet, but I am enjoying my work. The Hardings are good people, and I think I'm settling in well," Elias said. "I'm almost afraid that it is all going too well."

"Why would you say that?"

"I've not ever felt at home anywhere before," he admitted. "I've traveled around most of my life. But I could grow used to it here, I think."

"You wait until the snow starts to fall, then tell me you like it here," she said with a chuckle. "I've never known cold like it."

"You aren't the first person to warn me of the winters here."

"You will need a warm coat. If you don't yet have one, go and see Old Porter. He has the most incredible furs and skins, and his daughters make wonderful coats, hats, mittens, and gloves. You'll need them out on the mountain with the cattle."

"I shall do that," Elias said. "Thank you for the recommendation."

"I cannot tell you how glad I was to get mine," she said. "It is bitterly cold in the early hours when I get up to start the ovens."

"I can't imagine. In the South, we just don't have weather that bad," he said.

They drew closer to the waters of the creek. "What on earth is wrong with it?" he exclaimed when he took in the rusty red color staining the rocks and tinting the water.

"Iron Creek," she said with a shrug. "There's iron underground in these parts and it gets into the water. You can drink it, but it tastes like blood."

CHAPTER 15

September 21, 1890, Iron Creek, Minnesota

"I suppose that makes perfect sense," Mr. Groves said, shaking his head and looking a little embarrassed that he'd not thought of it himself. He looked at her quizzically. "You drink a lot of blood, to know that it tastes the same?"

"Enough," she said. "It is a common ingredient in cooking, after all. No man should waste any part of an animal he's killed."

"I heartily agree."

They walked along the banks of the creek. They didn't talk much, but it wasn't awkward. Once they had gotten past their initial nerves, it felt like they had known each other for years. There was a strange comfort in being in Mr. Groves' company that Marta rarely felt with anyone. She had it with

Emily and Mayor Winston, and even with Richard, but it wasn't something she was used to. She'd been let down by too many people in her life to trust easily, yet she did trust Mr. Groves.

He didn't just make her feel safe. He also made her feel excited and nervous and a cornucopia of emotions that she'd never felt before. It was rather strange to be so at ease with someone and yet so wary of them. It was most perplexing, and she wasn't entirely sure if she liked it. She vowed to ask Emily if that was how she had felt about Richard.

"You said that you only moved to Iron Creek last year?" he asked as they rounded a bend in the creek and came across a small pool with a tiny, finely pebbled beach where the children of Iron Creek often came in the summer to cool off and play in the water.

"I did. I came with Emily. She had met Richard while looking for her father, and they fell in love. He had moved here with his aunt, and she followed him."

"Would you follow a man for love?"

"If he asked me to, and if he cared for me as deeply as Richard loves Emily," Marta said simply. "But I would have a lot to lose if I left here now. I've made a life for myself. I have a share in two bakeries. I have an apprentice to train and friends who are closer to me than any family. It would have to be a very special man to make me leave." She watched his expression as she spoke and was glad to note that he actually seemed impressed by her words rather than upset by them. Too many men would expect a woman to follow them wherever they led, without argument. He needed to know now, before they grew any closer, that she was not that kind of woman.

"I'd not dare to presume to take you away from this place. After all, you have a much more successful career than my own," he said lightly. "Perhaps I should be the one to offer to follow you wherever you might go?"

"I'd not ask that of anyone. I would hope you would choose to stay here not just because I ask it of you but because you love it here, too."

"You still hope, having met me in person, that we will continue to get along?" he asked tentatively.

She smiled at him. "I do. I think it is going rather well so far, don't you?"

"I do. I like you, a lot." He paused. "I mean, I knew I liked you from your very first letter, but it is nice to see that you are the same person in the flesh as you were on paper. So many people are not."

"Likewise," she said. "You speak just as you write."

"I am glad you think so. I don't find writing to anyone easy, but it always felt like I was just having a conversation with you."

Marta moved to the edge of the water. The way he was looking at her with his intense green eyes was disconcerting and wonderful. It was as if he was trying to take in every aspect of her face so he would not ever forget it. He was so unnervingly handsome that to have his gaze so acutely focused on her felt strange. She wasn't used to receiving such attention. She picked up a couple of stones and skimmed them across the water, trying to calm her suddenly increasing heartbeat.

"Miss Pauling, I am very glad I came," he said, his voice coming from just behind her. She didn't dare look back, but she knew that he was standing just a pace or two away from her. "And I am very glad that we have met."

"Me too," she croaked, her mouth suddenly dry and her palms sweaty. "But perhaps we should make our way back to Emily and Richard's before we are late for lunch?"

They made their way back to the town, then passed through it, heading out toward the Balls' lovely home. Walking with Mr. Groves was definitely easier than having him look at her as intently as he had down by the creek.

"This is a lovely place," he said when they reached the house.

"It was almost derelict when Richard and his aunt found it," Marta told him. "They've had so much work done to it."

"Whoever did it has made it a lovely home."

"That was Geoffrey Drayton. Have you met him yet?"

"I think he was up at the Hardings' just yesterday, talking with Garrett about building a new barn. He seemed a good man."

"He is, and his wife, Jeannie, is the sweetest woman. She is a veritable force of nature, and she organizes all sorts of events for the town. She virtually raised all her sisters. When you go and visit Old Porter, you'll see most of them. They all still live there, with their husbands. Not one of them is like Jeannie. I suppose none of them bothers to do much because she was always there to take care of them and organize everything."

"Sounds like it must have been hard work for her."

"It must have been, but she'd never complain about it, or that they still need her now, even though she has her own babies to raise."

Marta led Mr. Groves around the back of the house and up onto the porch. "I'd love to have a garden one day," he said, looking out at the neat beds of the vegetable garden. His expression changed for a moment. It was hard to pinpoint what it meant, but he looked a little ashamed before he quickly composed himself. The change was so swift that she wouldn't have noticed it if she hadn't been watching him so closely. "I used to help an old friend in his garden when I was a boy, but I haven't had the chance to do much since," he explained quickly.

"I don't garden," she said. "I'd like to, but the bakery takes most of my time, and a garden needs more than I have to offer."

"Then I shall ensure our garden grows well," he said with a grin. "And you can turn everything I grow into something delicious to eat."

"That's a deal," she said, glad that whatever had upset

him before had passed. She also rather liked that he was already planning their life together, even if it had just been said as a joke. It meant he was thinking of how things would work between them, and she couldn't help feeling rather pleased about that.

Emily welcomed them into the kitchen. She and Mrs. Ball were setting the table. "Mr. Groves, if you'd like to go and join the menfolk, they're in Richard's study. The door to the left, off the hallway," Mrs. Ball said with a smile.

"Thank you, ma'am," he said, his Southern drawl even more pronounced than usual.

Emily looked fit to burst while she waited for him to be out of earshot. "So, how did it go?" she demanded as soon as they heard the click of the study door behind him.

"It was lovely. As easy as writing to him was," Marta said, taking a seat at the table. Emily placed a pan of potatoes in front of her.

"Mash those," she said, "and tell us all about it."

After adding butter, warm milk, salt, and a dash of pepper to them, Marta began to mash the potatoes. "Well, we just walked down by the creek for a while. We talked some, and we were quiet for some of the time, and it wasn't difficult at all."

Emily beamed. "He is terribly good-looking."

"Those eyes," Mrs. Ball said, sounding as dreamy as a young girl. "Edward had piercing eyes like that, though his were blue and not green."

"He is easy on the eye," Marta admitted. "But sometimes, those eyes are a little too much. They make me go all aflutter."

"They'd make any girl go weak at the knees," Emily said. "But it went well, and you like him. That is wonderful."

"It did, I do, and I only hope he feels the same way," Marta said wistfully.

They finished preparing the meal, then called the men through to serve it. Everyone sat around the table and soon they were all laughing and joking together, like any other Sunday lunchtime. Marta was pleased that Mr. Groves fit in so well with her friends. They were such an important part of her life, closer than her family had ever been. If they had disliked him, or him them, it would have been impossible to consider seeing him again.

She was even happier when he and Richard made plans to go for a ride together. Richard wanted to go and visit the Ojibwe settlement, and Mr. Groves had offered to help Dibikad and Garrett do some work Zaaga needed to get done before winter. She couldn't help feeling a little jealous that Richard would be the one to accompany them there, though. She'd love to visit the Ojibwe and learn more about the way they lived.

After a pleasant meal, they said their goodbyes to the Balls. Mayor Winston tactfully waited behind so that Mr. Groves could walk Marta home alone. They walked slowly, their bellies full of roasted beef and Marta's delicious potatoes. "Thank you for today," Mr. Groves said as they drew close to town.

"It was my pleasure," Marta said. "I enjoyed it, too."

"Your friends are wonderful people. Very warm and welcoming."

"That's Iron Creek for you."

"But none of you were from here originally," he pointed out.

"Most people in Iron Creek came here from somewhere else. Many met like us, via newspaper advertisements," Marta told him.

"Really? Until I started writing to you, I never really thought about how successful such advertisements might be."

"Oh, there are lots of mail-order couples here. We are a testament to the success of the matrimonial advertisement," Marta joked. "I only hope I don't ruin the run of luck the town has had." As soon as the words had come out of her mouth, she regretted saying them. She did not wish to put undue pressure upon Mr. Groves or their burgeoning friendship.

He simply smiled at her. "Neither do I," he said.

"Oh, I am glad," she said. "I am so happy that you are here."

"I am, too. And I would very much like to take you walking again next Sunday if that suits you."

"It does," Marta said eagerly. "I can hardly wait."

"Neither can I."

They reached Mayor Winston's impressive home all too soon. Marta did not want to say goodbye to him. It had been a wonderful day. They stopped at the gate, and she unlatched it and pushed it open, her hand trembling a little.

"Thank you for walking me home," she said with a smile. Then it struck her that he had no way to get back up the mountain. If he walked, it would be dark long before he made it up to the Hardings' place. "You have no horse."

"No, I came in the wagon with Katy and the children," he said with a wry smile. "I have a long walk ahead of me."

"You cannot walk it this late," she said. "Not without a lantern or a decent coat," she looked at the thin jacket he was wearing. It was perfect for a sunny fall afternoon, but not for a Minnesota fall night.

"I don't have any other choice," he said with a smile. "I didn't know I would be out so late. I assumed that I would be home long before now, but I don't regret it one bit, even if I am half-frozen by the time I get to the bunkhouse."

"You should take a horse from the public stable," Marta said. "You might make it before it gets dark that way."

"I'll not take a man from his family on a Sunday," Mr. Groves said. "Mr. Jenks works long enough hours as it is. But if you could perhaps lend me a lantern, I'd be grateful?" He gave her a warm smile that made her insides melt. He had stayed later than he had intended because of her. And now he was not complaining about the long walk back. It made her feel very wanted indeed.

"Wait here," she said. She ran into the pantry and found an old lantern at the back of one of the shelves. She filled it with oil quickly and lit it, then went back into the hallway, where she opened the hall closet and pulled out one of Mayor Winston's coats. It would be too short in the sleeves for Mr. Groves, but it would be better than what he had.

When she took the lantern and the coat outside, Mr. Groves was still standing where she had left him. He smiled when he saw her coming toward him. "You didn't need to," he said as she handed him the warm fur coat. "But I'm glad you did."

As she had expected, his hands and half his forearms poked out of the end of the coat, but Mayor Winston's round frame meant that it was just big enough around Mr. Groves' broad shoulders and slim torso.

"Well, goodnight," he said, yanking his shirt and jacket down to cover his wrists. "I shall see you next Sunday."

"Good night," she said.

He turned to go, then stopped. He bit his lip nervously, then leaned over the gate and pressed a kiss to her cheek. "It has been lovely," he said before turning and beginning his long walk back to the Hardings' place. Marta raised a hand to her cheek and grinned. It had been more than lovely. It had been perfect.

CHAPTER 16

September 26, 1890, the Ojibwe settlement, near Iron Creek, Minnesota

Dibikad grinned when the trio of men arrived in the Ojibwe village. "Welcome," he said. "I hope you're ready to work hard. Zaaga has a list of things she wants doing, and it is as long as your horse is tall."

Garrett chuckled. "It's good to see that my mother intends to make good use of our time here," he said. He embraced Dibikad, who hugged him back tightly, then introduced him to Richard.

Richard and Elias got down from their horses and hitched them to a nearby post. "So, what are we here to do?" Elias asked Dibikad as the two men shook hands. They'd met a couple of times at Garrett's place and got on well.

"There are four dwellings that need new roofs, and we

need to build four more. Several families have joined us this year," Dibikad explained. "Obviously, everyone pitches in to help, but there are all the usual chores to be done as well, so nobody has as much time to offer as they'd like."

"We're glad to help," Garrett assured him. "And it will be interesting for Richard and Elias to see how the Ojibwe make their homes."

"I'm looking forward to it," Elias said. Richard nodded his agreement. He was staring around the settlement with wide eyes. Elias nudged him and whispered, "Don't stare." he whispered.

"I'm sorry," Richard said. "I've never seen anything like it before."

Dibikad smiled at his honesty. "I know that your people wonder how we live through the winter in our birch bark houses, but they're remarkably warm and cozy inside. Do you want to see? Zaaga told me to take you all to hers for some tea before we get started."

He led the way toward one of the larger houses, where Zaaga welcomed them and gave them some raspberry leaf tea. It was delicious and something Elias had never tried before. Richard obviously hadn't either, and he asked Zaaga lots of questions about it and her house. She patiently answered his questions with amusement. Elias wondered how she managed that because he'd have been utterly fed up with such an interrogation within moments, but he had to admit that he was glad Richard was so curious as he, too, found Zaaga's answers very interesting.

When they had drunk their tea, she shoved them all outside and gave them and the men of the Ojibwe their tasks for the day. Elias was part of a group assigned to raising the new birch bark houses. He watched the men around him and copied the way they did everything. Before long, he was almost as adept as his fellow workers, though he doubted he'd ever be quite as quick and accurate using an ax as they were.

By the time the sun was beginning to set, four new dwellings had been built and the older dwellings had been re-roofed. Men had come and gone through the day. Only Garrett, Richard, Elias, and Dibikad had been there through-out. But everyone who had helped, joined them around a large campfire, where Zaaga and the other women served them all hearty meals and beer they had brewed themselves.

After the meal, people began to tell stories, then sing and play musical instruments, and it wasn't long before they started dancing. It was a wonderful and unexpected party. Elias could hardly wait until Sunday to tell Marta all about his experience. He knew that she would want to hear all about it. Dibikad sank down on the ground beside him. "You don't dance?" he asked breathlessly, having led the dancing from the start.

"Not really," Elias admitted. "I'm a little too clumsy, but there's someone I'd like to be able to dance for."

"One of the girls in Iron Creek?"

"Yes. Miss Pauling."

"The baker? Oh my, you'd be a lucky man indeed to win her heart," Dibikad said with a grin. "Everyone here loves Marta's food."

"You all shop in town?" Elias asked, surprised at Dibikad's enthusiasm.

"We have to buy things somewhere."

"I can't imagine that happening in New Mexico, where I lived. The local tribes lived very separate lives from the White people."

"So I hear," Dibikad said. "Not everyone who came to this country uninvited was so gracious to those already here, but our people have been lucky. And we have real, living ties to your community in Garrett, Nelson, and their children."

"I'm glad that you are able to live without fear of us," Elias said.

"I didn't say that," Dibikad said with a grin. "We're still wary. There's no telling when things might change, but things are good for now."

"I think that is wise," Elias agreed. His day among the Ojibwe had taught him a lot, but his lifetime living further south, where things were still fractious between the White men and the local tribes, had shown him how little it took to destroy any tentative peace between the two peoples.

"You're safe," Dibikad assured him.

"I do hope so," Elias said, but he wasn't just thinking

about whether relations between the town and the settlement would remain good. He knew that his life here, one he was coming to enjoy more each and every day, could be destroyed in a moment. He'd not heard anything from Mr. Hill, so he prayed that Hanley was satisfied that he'd run Elias off, but letters could go missing. He might not find out that his world was about to collapse around him in time to do anything about it.

And now there was Miss Pauling. He already cared for her greatly. He never wanted to disappoint her or cause her any pain, and he knew that her learning about his past would do both. He could not imagine telling her, but he dreaded how she would feel if she found out from someone else. Every day that he heard nothing from New Mexico, he started to breathe a little easier, but he continued to pray that his past would not catch up with him here. He did not want to have to confess to it, not now. It was too late for it to have been an innocent mistake, just something he'd forgotten to mention. If it came out now, it would ruin everything.

As his thoughts began to spiral, the joys of the evening began to fade away. Suddenly, he felt afraid again, a feeling he'd begin to feel less and less as he'd begun to settle in Iron Creek. He'd never cared much for anywhere he'd lived before, and Nev and Warden Greenslade had been his only real friends over the years. But here, he had been made welcome. He was building friendships with Garrett, with Richard, with Miss Pauling, and he liked it here.

Dibikad pulled himself to his feet and began to dance again. Garrett took his place beside Elias, looking amused to see his friend dancing wildly.

"Thank you for your help today," he said, turning to grin at Elias. "I'm glad you're here. And I know the cattle are glad that I'm no longer trying to work out what they need." Elias forced a laugh, but Garrett was a perceptive man and he caught that Elias wasn't entirely comfortable. "What is it?"

Elias sighed. If he told Garrett now, he could lose his position and be driven out of town that very night. But if he didn't, he might burst. He had to know that somebody here knew who he really was and still accepted him. If Garrett could not accept his past, then he knew there would be no chance that Miss Pauling would.

"I should have told you this before," he said cautiously, "but I was afraid you wouldn't give me a chance to prove myself."

Garrett sat upright, his expression changing rapidly from one of amusement to one of concern. "Whatever it is, you can tell me. It won't change things," he said firmly.

"It will," Elias said. "But it is best if I tell you, anyway."

Garrett gave him a puzzled look but did not argue any further. "Then tell me," he said simply.

Elias quickly told his tale, from the very start to the reason he'd come to Iron Creek. Garrett stayed perfectly quiet and still as he listened. At the end of his story, Elias stopped speaking and waited nervously for Garrett to react.

"Well," he said, shaking his head and giving Elias a slap on the back. "If that is all, I think we can put that in the past, where it belongs."

"You're sure?" Elias asked. "Many men wouldn't."

"Elias, you work harder than any man I've ever known. You have told me about something that you did not need to tell me, something that happened when you were a boy. You are a man, and it is time for you to stop blaming yourself for your father's actions. From what you just said, he wouldn't have wanted that. You're making a life for yourself here, away from all that. And you deserve to do so. I'll tell you all about my past one day. I was just as reluctant to let myself be happy, but I'm so glad I learned to let others in. Katy turned me and my life around."

"You had a troubled past?" Elias asked, incredulous at such a revelation.

"Every man does. Anyone who says they do not is a liar," Garrett said. "None of us is an angel, none of us is the devil. We're just trying to survive in this world, doing the best we can with the hand that we've been dealt."

"You changed your hand, then?"

"I did, and you are doing the same."

Elias felt his heart lift a little, knowing that there was at least one person in Iron Creek who knew of his past. It was cathartic admitting to it rather than letting it fester inside him, but he still wasn't sure he could bring himself to tell Miss Pauling. He was more hopeful now that she would hear him out, but though Garrett was happy to accept him as he was because of his own history, he doubted that Miss Pauling would see things the same way. She was a good, Christian woman, and he doubted that she had ever done anything sinful in her life. How could she possibly understand? On the other hand, perhaps he was being too pessimistic. Miss Pauling was kind and generous. Surely, she would forgive him for something so very long ago?

But it was not the time to let his worries overwhelm him. He tried his best to enjoy the rest of the evening with the Ojibwe, even letting Dibikad and Garrett drag him up to dance. They taught him a few steps and he was soon whooping and whirling around the fire with everyone else. It was very freeing to dance with the sound of drums rumbling through his entire body. When people began to drift away from the fire, to go to their beds, the three men mounted their horses and made their way back toward Garrett's place.

"You can stay the night, Richard," Garrett said when they reached the yard. "There's a bed in the bunkhouse."

"Thank you. I think I'd fall asleep in the saddle if I try to go a step further," Richard said.

They all dismounted and led their horses into the barn. Each of them removed his mount's saddle and bridle, rubbed the animal down, then led it into a stall with a full trough of hay.

When Garrett headed to the farmhouse, Elias led Richard to the bunkhouse. "It's cozy," Richard noted as he peered inside.

Elias put a finger to his lips. "Shh, the others will be asleep," he whispered. He pulled off his boots and crept softly past the sleeping bodies of his fellow hands. Richard followed him to the spare bed at the end of the bunkhouse.

"They're comfier than they look," Elias whispered, nodding at the narrow cot beds.

"I'm glad of that," Richard whispered with a grin. He collapsed onto the bed and pulled the blankets over his still-clothed body.

Elias did the same but lay staring at the ceiling for a while. Soon enough, he heard even breaths coming from Richard's cot. He could hear Dirk's gentle snores and Paul's occasional bursts of chatter at the other end of the bunkhouse. Such sounds didn't usually bother him at all, but tonight they kept him wide awake. At least he had told the truth to Garrett and his past had not worried his employer one bit, but Garrett was not the only one he needed to be truthful with. Even before he had come to Iron Creek, his feelings for Miss Pauling had been strong, but he'd realized that she was the only woman for him as soon as he'd met her in person. He loved her big blue eyes, her long, soft blonde hair, her cheeky sense of humor, and her romantic heart.

He had to find the courage to tell Miss Pauling. If he did not, how could he know if she truly loved him as he was?

And more to the point, how could he let her love him not knowing his true story? When he finally closed his eyes, he was determined that he would tell her when they went walking on Sunday. It was the very least that he could do. She deserved to know, even if it lost him the only woman that he had ever let himself fall in love with.

CHAPTER 17

*S*unday, September 28, 1890, Iron Creek, Minnesota

It had been a busy week in the bakery, but the time had dragged unusually slowly. Marta could hardly wait to see Mr. Groves again, and he'd been on her mind in every spare moment. She dressed and pinned her hair carefully at the front, leaving her gentle curls to fall down over her shoulders. When she felt she looked as lovely as she could, she prayed that the day would be as magical as the previous Sunday had been. She could still feel the warmth of his lips where he had kissed her cheek, and it made her flush with happiness every time she thought of it.

The church was already packed with people when she and Mayor Winston arrived. Emily, Richard, and Mrs. Ball were seated in the front pew. Mayor Winston beamed as he saw the older woman, and he immediately took the seat next to her. Marta would not be surprised if they made an announcement of an intention to be wed before long. They spent all the time they could together and seemed utterly smitten with one another. She knew that both Emily and Richard approved of the match, though Mrs. Ball had been a little reluctant at first. She did not wish to seem hasty or for others to think that she had forgotten her beloved husband so soon.

Marta looked around as she moved into the pew and sat down beside Emily, but she could see no sign of Mr. Groves or the Hardings. She could only presume that they were a little late in arriving. The service was as lovely as ever. Father Paul was an excellent priest, and his sermons were always interesting and thought-provoking. But there was still no sign of Mr. Groves by the end of it.

"Have you seen Katy or Garrett?" she asked Mary Jelli-coe, who was trying, unsuccessfully, to stop her twins from chasing each other around the churchyard, yelling names at one another. Samuel and Thomas were too old to be such tearaways, but it seemed that age was not slowing them down in any way. Hector, their father, said they were as rambunctious now as they had been as three-year-olds, and he and Mary were permanently exhausted by them.

"I haven't, sorry, Marta," Mary said. "Boys, stop that this instant. You're too old for such nonsense. I'll not let you have any of Marta's delicious cherry pie if you carry on this way. On Sunday, of all days." The twins stopped running but stood sullenly kicking at the dirt on the ground before they started to poke each other again. "Right, home with you, now," Mary said firmly, taking each of them by the ear and dragging them away. It was rather amusing to see tiny Mary lugging her two rapidly growing sons, who towered over her, along Main Street.

Marta waited until everyone had gone, but there was still no sign of Mr. Groves or the Hardings. She couldn't help feeling a little concerned. It wasn't like Katy to miss church, even if Garrett didn't always attend with her and the children. She decided to go up the mountain to see what was wrong and to find out if there was anything she could do to help.

It was a long walk, even on a day with fine weather, but there was a light drizzle that had her soaked to the skin before she'd even made it halfway up to the rambling farmhouse. By the time she reached it, she was exhausted and couldn't help thinking that she had made a dreadful mistake. Perhaps Mr. Groves simply hadn't wanted to meet her, or maybe Katy had needed help with the little ones. Perhaps everyone was sick.

Nervously, she knocked on the door of the bunkhouse. She couldn't hear anyone, but that didn't mean there wasn't someone taking a nap inside. But even when she knocked again, much louder, there was no answer. She crossed the yard, stepped up onto the wide porch, and rapped on the front door of the house. She listened intently, trying to hear something inside, but the place was eerily quiet. Something was wrong, she was sure of it.

She went into the barn and saw Jet in his stall. She stroked his handsome nose. "Where's your master," she asked him. "D'you know?" He nickered softly as she patted his neck. It was as if he was saying that of course he did. "Think you could take me to him?" He gave a little harrumph as if such a task would be all too easy.

Marta laughed. She must have lost her wits. Here she was, talking to a horse as if he could understand every word she said. Despite her doubts, she still saddled him and mounted up, then led him out into the yard and toward the paddocks. She could see for quite a long way from there, but there was nothing except grass and trees for miles and miles.

Jet neighed loudly, then suddenly took off at a gallop, going northwards. "I hope you know where you're going," Marta said, clinging on for dear life. Jet was most certainly not taking directions from her – he was going his own way – and that seemed strange, given that Mr. Groves had told her that Jet was a highly trained animal who obeyed the lightest of touches.

He led her further up the mountain than she'd been before, then along a narrow path with a steep drop on either side of it, then down a heavily wooded path. From just ahead, she heard the sound of a child's scream, then the deep sound of Garrett Harding's voice. "Calm down, Jacob, we'll get you all out."

Marta urged Jet forwards. Garrett was standing above a narrow fissure in the rocks, peering down anxiously. Dirk and Paul, his shepherds, were tying a rope to a large oak tree. Dirk yanked on it hard to make sure it was tied tightly, then they let it down into the hole.

"Garrett, what's going on?" Marta asked.

"Katy and Jacob went out for a walk before church this morning, and Jacob fell down into the crevasse, here," Garrett explained. "She tried to reach in and pull him out but fell down with him instead."

"Oh my!" Marta exclaimed. "That's terrible. How did you know to come here?"

"She sent the other children back to the house to find help."

"That was brave of them, to go all that way."

"They were pretty scared when they found me, were worried that they'd never see Katy and Jacob again. Mr. Groves was great with them. He played with them and took their minds off it so we could get ready to head out."

"Where are they now? There's nobody at the farm."

"I asked him to take them to my mother. She'll take care of the little ones until we're sure that Jacob and Katy are safe." He paused, then looked at her intently. "What made you come here? You don't often come this far up the mountain."

"I was worried when none of you were in church, and it seems that I was right to be so," Marta said. "I saddled Jet, and he led me right here."

"He's too clever by half, that horse," Garrett said with a rueful grin.

"What can I do to help?"

"We're going to lower down the rope and pull them up one at a time," Garrett said. "Katy said she's hurt her leg pretty bad, and Jacob has a nasty bump on his head. They'll need a doctor, so could you go and fetch Dr. Anna?"

"I'll go straight away," Marta said without hesitation.

She rode swiftly back to Iron Creek, delighted that Jet obeyed her every command this time. He needed the very lightest of touches to turn, slow, or go faster, and he was a delight to ride. Mr. Groves was lucky to have such a fine animal. It was no wonder he hadn't wanted to leave Jet behind when he came here. As soon as they reached the clinic, she banged loudly on the door. There was no answer, which meant they'd had no serious patients over the week- end, so Marta ran down the street to Dr. Anna's house and banged loudly on her door.

Alec Jenks opened the door. He was a hulking brute to look at, but he was one of the gentlest men Marta had ever known. "Is Dr. Anna home?" she asked him quickly. "Katy and Jacob fell into a crevasse."

"Anna, you're needed," he yelled up the stairs. He turned back to Marta. "How tight is the crevasse?"

"It looked very narrow," she told him. "I don't rightly know how either of them fell into it. It didn't look big enough."

"I'll fetch some tools," he said before grabbing his coat and hurrying across the street to the smithy. By the time Dr. Anna had come downstairs with her black medical bag in hand, he was waiting outside with a small wagon.

Dr. Anna heaved herself up onto the seat beside her husband. "Lead the way," she said, her face anxious. "We'll be right behind you."

"You'll not get a wagon along the last trails," Marta warned them, "but you'll be able to go most of the way."

Alec nodded, and they set off. Marta suddenly felt terribly weary as they passed through the Hardings' farmyard and continued up the trail. She was surprised to see another wagon already parked at the end of the track that was passable for wagons. Alec grabbed a length of thick rope and a large bag that clanked and clattered as they walked quickly toward the crevasse. Marta's heart soared with joy at the sight of Mr. Groves pulling on a rope with Dirk and Paul.

"Stop," Garrett told them, frowning at the spot where the rope dropped over the rocks into the crevasse. "It just keeps fraying."

"You need this," Alec said. He threw his rope to Dirk, who caught it and then staggered a little at the weight of it. "Tie it to the tree, like you did the other one." He turned back to Garrett. "And you need this." He tipped out the contents of the bag, which turned out to be a number of sturdy metal poles and a couple of pulleys. Alec erected them quickly and fed the free end of the rope through the pulley, then checked it was running smoothly.

"Now, we can lower it down and it won't fray on the rocks," Alec said.

Garrett slapped him on the back and sighed heavily. "Thank you, my friend."

"Might be easier if someone goes down there," Alec said. "You want to be sure that the ropes are tied good and tight around their waists. If they fall from the rope, they'll be badly injured."

"I'm not sure any of us will fit down there," Garrett said, peering at the crevasse.

"I'll go," Marta volunteered bravely. "I'm bigger than Katy, but I'm the smallest of all of us.

"Can you tie a good knot?" Mr. Groves asked, handing her the rope.

"I lived on a farm for most of my young life. I can tie a knot as well as any of you," she retorted. She took the rope and bound it around her own waist.

Alec yanked on it, hard. He was incredibly strong, and Marta felt as though he might actually pull her over, but the knot held tight. "She can tie a knot," he confirmed.

"I don't think you should," Mr. Groves said, his eyes full

of concern. "It is dark down there, and if you should fall as well..." His voice tailed off.

"I shall be fine," she assured him. "I've been in far stickier situations as a girl."

Reluctantly, he took her to the edge of the fissure in the rock. She peered into the darkness but couldn't see a thing. "We'll lower you down slowly. If you get scared or think you'll get stuck, just yell and we'll pull you right back up," he said as he handed her some matches and a candle.

She tucked them into the bodice of her gown, which made him grin unexpectedly. She grinned back, nodded, and glanced over at Garrett, who was looking pale and afraid. "I'll have them back up with you in no time," she assured him.

CHAPTER 18

September 28, 1890, Iron Creek, Minnesota

Slowly, inch by inch, the men above lowered Marta into the crevasse. Her belly was a mass of knots, but she took some deep breaths and looked up rather than down. The journey down seemed very long, and she had to squeeze through some tight cracks, but she eventually felt her feet touch the ground of the cave below. She stopped looking up and looked around her. In the gloom, she could make out two figures sitting propped up against the wall close by.

"Katy, Jacob, it's going to be alright," she promised them when she lit the candle and saw their dirty, scared faces.

As Garrett had said, Jacob had a big lump on his head, and there was a trickle of blood over his cheek. Marta checked him over quickly and was reassured that, other than a few small cuts and bruises, he seemed fine everywhere else. She quickly unknotted the rope around her waist and tied it tightly around his.

"I'm going to call up to your daddy," she told him calmly. "And he is going to pull you up, but you'll need to help him a little by walking up the rock with your feet and hands so you can make your way around all the bits that jut out. Can you do that?"

He nodded solemnly. "I can," he said. "But shouldn't Mama go first? She's hurt real bad."

"I'll get your mama ready to follow you right up," Marta promised him. "But you go on up to your daddy now."

Marta called up to Garrett and Mr. Groves, and they began to slowly reel the rope back in. As she'd told him to, Jacob walked up the wall with his hands and feet, making sure the rope didn't snag on the rocks and that he wasn't pulled up too quickly into any of the sharp edges.

Once he was out of sight, she turned back to Katy. "You don't look so good," she said, kneeling beside her. Katy was pale and had a large gash on her leg. She'd lost quite a lot of blood and could barely stand. Marta yanked a strip off her petticoat and wrapped it around Katy's leg. "It is going to hurt, a lot," she warned her. "You'll have to do what I told Jacob to do. The crevasse is not nice and straight, so they can't just pull you up. Can you do that?"

"I'm tougher than I look," Katy said through gritted teeth, as the rope came back down the shaft. "I can do it."

Marta tied the rope around Katy's waist, then helped her

up onto her feet. Katy sagged against her and exhaled sharply. "I know it hurts," Marta said, "but you are doing great. I'd be screaming like a baby in your place."

"They say that there's nothing more painful than childbirth," Katy joked, "but I'd give anything to be in labor rather than going through this."

Marta grinned at her. "Dr. Anna is right above us. She'll get you back on your feet in no time, and I'm sure there will be something in that little black bag of hers to help with the pain."

Katy gave her a brave smile. "Let's get it over with," she said, her voice faltering just a little.

"She's on her way," Marta called up, and watched as the rope began to tauten. She bit her lip as she watched Katy try and gain a foothold on the rocks, to guide herself up, but her injured right leg was making it much harder for her. Nevertheless, she somehow managed to guide herself up and out of sight. Some moments later, Marta heard a small cry and guessed Katy had reached the top. The rope was soon thrown back down to her, and when it reached her she tied it around her own waist and started to make her own way back into the light.

When she reached the top, Mr. Groves grabbed her and held her tightly. She could feel his heart beating, loud and fast, against her cheek. He had been afraid for her, and that meant he cared for her, and that made everything around them almost disappear for her. She looked up into his eyes and knew, without him saying a word, that he loved her just as much as she loved him. But it was not the time for such fancies, as much as she longed to stay here in his arms forever.

Reluctantly, she pulled away and hurried to Katy's side. Jacob was sitting beside his mother, holding tightly to her hand. Garrett was holding her body upright against his own while Dr. Anna, kneeling by her leg, unwrapped the petticoat bandage and inspected the wound.

"It's nasty, but we can sew you up," the doctor said with a smile.

"Mama is going to be alright?" Jacob asked.

"She is, and so will you be, once you've both had a good night's rest in the clinic," Dr. Anna said firmly.

"What about the other children," Katy said, turning her head, to see her husband.

"They're with Zaaga," Garrett said softly. "I'll send Dirk to let her know you're both safe." Dirk nodded and disappeared immediately.

Katy sighed and closed her eyes almost immediately after Dr. Anna had placed a couple of drops of laudanum on her tongue. "I'll carry her to the cart," Alec said, lifting Katy up as if she weighed no more than a feather.

"We'll bring everything back down to the smithy for you," Mr. Groves told Alec as he helped Garrett to his feet. "Go with your wife, Sir, she needs you now, as does your boy."

Garrett picked Jacob up and followed Alec and Dr. Anna back up the path to where they'd left the wagons.

It was starting to get dark by the time they had finished coiling the ropes and packing up the winch and pulley. Paul hoisted the heavy bag onto his back and set off as Marta helped Mr. Groves put the large, heavy coil of rope over his shoulder and across his body. Marta did the same with the smaller rope that they had been using when she'd first arrived, then they walked back up the path toward the Hardings' wagon and Jet.

"Hey boy," Mr. Groves said when he saw his horse waiting patiently. "You did great today." He patted Jet's neck, and the horse nuzzled at his pockets, looking for a treat. "No carrots there now, boy, but I'll make sure you get lots when we get back."

"Want me to ride him back?" Paul asked. "You can take Miss Pauling back home in the wagon."

"Thank you," Mr. Groves said. "I'd be grateful. I can rub him down when I get back."

"I'll do that," Paul said and gestured towards the other horse. "You'll have old Walter there to deal with. And I'll make sure Jet gets plenty of carrots in with his oats."

"He'll never want me to ride him again," Mr. Groves said with a chuckle as Paul bounced up into the saddle and began to make his way back to the Hardings' place.

Once Marta had thrown her rope in the back of the wagon and heaved her weary body up onto the bench, Mr.

Groves climbed up and took the reins. He was about to drive off when Marta's body began to shake. "What is wrong?" he asked her. "Did you hurt yourself?"

"No, I am quite well," she assured him. "I can't think why I suddenly feel so peculiar."

"You've had quite an ordeal," he said, pulling a blanket out from a box under the seat. "Wrap that around you, and we'll get you home. Mayor Winston can give you some hot, sweet tea and then you can go to bed. I'd suggest that you don't open the bakery tomorrow so you can get some much-needed rest."

She nodded, but the idea of not opening the bakery was positively impossible to her. She was suddenly very, very tired, so she let her head rest upon Mr. Groves' shoulder and closed her eyes. It wasn't long before she was asleep. She woke with a start when he brought the wagon to a halt outside Mayor Winston's house.

"You're home," he said softly. He pressed a gentle kiss to her forehead, then got down from the wagon, ran around it, and lifted her down.

Her legs felt like jelly, and she collapsed against him as he set her down on the ground. He whisked her up into his arms and carried her up the garden path. Mayor Winston opened the door, looking worried.

"I wondered where she'd gone. She disappeared after church, and nobody knew a thing," he said. "I'll have to send word to Emily. She was so scared when the two of you did not come to lunch."

"Miss Pauling is a heroine," Mr. Groves said with a doting smile. "She saved Katy and Jacob Harding from a crevasse today. She is very tired and weak. She needs her bed."

"Take her up. First door to the right," Mayor Winston said. "What can I do?"

"She needs some hot, sweet tea and some cake if you have any," Mr. Groves said.

"I shall fetch it immediately." The mayor hurried off to the kitchen, then turned back. "But it would be improper for you to take her to her bedroom alone. Perhaps I should take her upstairs and you should fetch the refreshments."

"I don't mean to be rude, Sir," Mr. Groves said with a weary smile, "but I doubt you could lift her all that way. And as I sincerely hope that Miss Pauling will soon be my wife, there cannot be too much that is improper in my taking her upstairs and leaving her on her bed, fully dressed, can there?"

Mayor Winston flushed a little and beamed. "No, I suppose not," he said. "Ooh, another wedding in the family. How very wonderful."

Marta stared at Mr. Groves' face as he took her up the stairs. He'd most definitely just said that he intended to make her his wife, yet he'd not asked her. He'd not even told her he loved her, but he had been afraid for her, and she so wanted it to be true. He laid her down tenderly on her bed and turned to leave the room.

"Don't go," she said. "Did you mean it?"

"What?"

"That you intend to marry me. Or did you say it just so that Mayor Winston would not get himself all worked up over propriety?"

He smiled and moved back to the bed. He perched on the very edge of it and took her hands in his. "Oh, I meant it."

"Then I really do think that it is time that you stopped calling me Miss Pauling," she said with a grin.

"I would be delighted to, as long as you will call me Elias."

"Elias," she said, dreamily, falling back against her pillow.

He smiled. "Will you marry me?" he asked, sounding a little concerned. "Or have I been entirely too presumptuous? It is just that I love you more than anything or anyone, and I want to make a life with you."

"Oh," Marta said, sitting back upright. "That is really rather wonderful because I want to make a life with you, too. And I love you."

"You do?" he asked, looking incredulous. "Well, I'll be…"

"Will you speak with Father Paul as soon as possible?" Marta asked with a grin. Suddenly, she no longer felt tired or out of sorts. She was soaring, on top of the world, as happy as a girl could possibly be.

Mayor Winston appeared in the doorway with a large silver tray in his hands. On it was a pot of tea, some cups and saucers, and three slices of cake. He put it down on the dresser and poured everyone a cup of hot, sweet tea.

"You don't have to tell me about it, my dear," he said to Marta. "But I am very proud of you."

"I will tell you," Marta promised. "But in the morning. Could you possibly send word to Gertie that she is to open up alone tomorrow? And that, yes, I am sure that she is capable of doing so. I think I shall be taking Mr. Groves' excellent advice and sleeping all day."

She beamed at her husband-to-be, who grinned back.

"Sir, I know you are not Miss Pauling's father, but I know that she thinks of you as a father figure, and as such, I believe it would only be fit and proper to ask you for her hand in marriage," Elias said.

"I know better than to try to tell dear Marta what to think or who to love, but I am happy to give you my blessing if she wishes to be your wife."

"Oh, I do want to be," Marta said eagerly. She flung her arms around the bemused-looking mayor's neck. "And you will walk me down the aisle, will you not?"

He blushed all the way up his neck and into his cheeks, obviously as pleased as punch. "I should be delighted, my dear. I should be delighted."

CHAPTER 19

October 30, 1890, Iron Creek, Minnesota

Father Paul had been delighted to arrange their wedding, but they'd had to wait an entire month as he was already fully booked with all manner of ceremonies and engagements that he refused to postpone. Elias had not minded, too much. A month was such a short time to have to wait when it meant that he would get to have Marta as his wife for the rest of his days. Yet the days had dragged terribly, and he had begun to fear that this day might never come.

Now that it had finally dawned, his heart felt light. He had his secrets, but he had been in Iron Creek for many months now. If his past was going to catch up with him, then it stood to reason that it would have done so by now. He hoped never to have to tell Marta about the scared little boy who had just wanted to please his father and the mess that had gotten him into.

Garrett knocked on the door of the bunkhouse. "You ready for your big day?" he asked with a grin as he stepped inside.

"I've been ready since I came to Iron Creek," Elias said.

"Does she know about what you told me?"

Elias frowned. "No, she doesn't. I've asked myself over and over what good it would serve for her to know, and I am certain that it would not be useful to either of us."

"I can understand that, but I'm not sure what kind of a start you're making if you cannot tell her the truth about who you are and the trials and tribulations that made you the man she loves."

"I know you are right," Elias said with a sigh. "But I am too afraid to lose her."

"Marta's not like most. I doubt she'd judge you too harshly, but you know her better than I do." He grinned. "But there is something else that may ruin your life together before it has even started."

"There is?" Elias said, puzzled. He was sure he had thought of everything. He had a new suit with a gold ring in the pocket to put on Marta's finger later that day.

"Where are the two of you going to live?" Garrett asked. "She's not going to want to live in a bunkhouse."

Elias sank down onto his bed and clapped his hands over his face. It was true, he'd not given that a moment's thought.

"What am I going to do? I can't bring her here on her wedding night. And I can't presume that Mayor Winston would be so kind as to let us live with him."

"Come with me," Garrett said, beckoning to him. He led Elias around the back of the farm buildings, along a narrow path between the paddocks, and through a small thicket of trees. "How do you like the view here?" he asked as they looked out over the landscape before them.

Elias shook his head. "It is beautiful." Garrett tapped him on the shoulder and pointed behind them. Nestled against the trees was a large cabin. "Who lives there?"

"You do," Garrett said. "I owe you and Marta everything. Both of you were there when I needed friends the most, and Marta brought my boy and my wife back to me, safe and sound. This place is yours for as long as you want to live here."

Elias shook his head, blinking back tears. He could not believe that anyone would offer him such generosity. "I do not know how to repay you."

"No, Elias. As I said, this is your payment, and Marta's, for what you have already done for me, for Jacob, for Katy. There is nothing more you could ever give me than the lives of my loved ones." He slapped Elias on the back affectionately. "And now we had best get you to the church on time."

They made their way back to the rambling farmhouse, where Katy and the children were waiting in the wagon. Katy beamed at him and patted the bench next to her. "You look very handsome," she said as he took the seat beside her and Garrett climbed into the back with his children. "Marta is a lucky girl."

"I am the lucky one," he insisted.

"And you just remember that," Garrett joked.

As the wagon trundled down the mountain, they listened to the birdsong and marveled that the day was bright and warm for the season. October could be bitterly cold, and Elias hadn't forgotten Marta's warning to get a coat from Old Porter before the winter came. He'd not found time to do so yet, but he would. He had no desire to freeze to death up here.

The sound of hoofbeats on the path ahead made Elias' spine prickle. He did not know why, but horses riding at speed up a road that only had one real destination could only mean trouble. He stopped the wagon when Sheriff Matt Hansen rode into view with two deputies flanking him on either side.

"How can we help you, Matt?" Garrett asked, standing up in the back of the wagon. "We'll be late for Elias' wedding if we tarry here too long."

"I'm sorry, Elias, but I have to take you in," the sheriff said. Elias stared at him, unable to speak. His worst fears were coming true, and on the day all his dreams should have been.

"For what?" Garrett asked. "Elias is a law-abiding member of our community. I'll vouch for him, and you know how I feel about lawbreakers. I was your deputy, remember."

"I do, Garrett, and I cannot tell you how sorry I am, but the warrant is out for his arrest. I cannot just ignore it. If I ignore every warrant that comes to me from other states, if every sheriff did the same, criminals would go free all over the country."

"What am I wanted for, Sheriff Hansen?" Elias said softly, his voice hoarse with fear.

"Murder," Sheriff Hansen said. "A man was killed in New Mexico, at around the time you left. There's a witness, apparently. Said there was no doubt in his mind that it was you."

"His name wouldn't happen to be Hanley, would it?" Elias asked bitterly. Hanley's influence reached further than Elias could ever have imagined if he had managed to ruin his life even here.

"I don't know. All I have is the warrant for your arrest," Matt said sadly. "Now, will you come quietly or are you going to make trouble?"

"I'll come quietly," Elias said. He got down from the wagon and stood by the sheriff's horse. He turned back to Garrett and Katy. "Tell Marta I am sorry. I'll write to her if I can, once I know more."

"What are you talking about?" Garrett said. "I'll send Richard to you straight away. He'll get to the bottom of this.

I know you wouldn't kill a man. I refuse to believe it, and Marta won't believe it either."

"Thank you," Elias said. "Just make sure she's alright. Look after her for me."

Katy nodded, but tears poured down her cheeks as Matt told Elias to mount up behind him and they rode away.

KATY BURST into Mayor Winston's house and ran straight up the stairs to Marta's room. Emily was just helping her into her dress.

"Marta, sit down. I have something to tell you," Katy said.

"What is it? Has something happened to Elias? Is he not coming? Does he not love me after all?" Marta said, feeling panicked. Her heart felt as though it was beating in her head, it was so loud.

"Sit down," Katy said firmly.

Marta perched nervously on the edge of her bed, and Katy kneeled in front of her. "Marta, he's not coming. But it is not because he does not want to." She paused as if searching for the right words. "I don't know how to say this, so I'll just say it quickly." Marta nodded that she should. "We were on our way down the mountain. Elias wanted to be at the church early. He didn't want anything to go wrong."

"And?" Emily asked, as impatient as Marta was to hear what could possibly have gone so wrong.

"And Sheriff Hansen came and arrested him. For murder," Katy blurted out.

"Murder?" Emily gasped.

"Murder?" Marta echoed. "But he is the kindest, sweetest man. He could not hurt a fly, much less kill a man."

"There must be some mistake. I shall send Richard to the sheriff's office immediately," Emily said, reaching for her coat.

"Garrett has already gone to him," Katy assured her. "I'm sure there must be some terrible mistake, but Elias was strangely resigned to it all."

"He did not fight? Did not protest his innocence?" Marta asked, baffled by such a notion.

"Not really, he asked about a man called Hanley, but he just went with Sheriff Hansen quietly," Katy said. "He just made us vow to take care of you and make sure you are alright."

"I'm going to the sheriff now," Marta said. She pulled a shawl from the chair by her bed and hurried downstairs before anyone could stop her.

She ran across the street and barged into the sheriff's office. "Where is he?" she demanded.

Sheriff Hansen gave her a sad look. "You look lovely, Marta. I am so sorry to have ruined your wedding."

"Then you should have at least waited to arrest him until

after the ceremony," she said pointedly. "He wasn't going to run anywhere."

"I suppose you're right," he said with a slightly rueful shrug. "But it's my job. I'll be taking him to Santa Fe on the next train."

"I want to see him," she demanded.

Sheriff Hansen took her around the back to the cells. Elias looked peculiarly small behind the heavy iron bars. She rushed to them. He stood up when he saw her, but he did not move any closer.

"Elias, talk to me," she demanded. "Whatever is happening?"

"I should have told you everything from the start," he said sadly. His usually intense eyes looked dull and tired, and his broad shoulders were slumped.

"Told me what?" she asked. "What is it that I don't know?"

He looked up at her, his expression pained. "I wanted it all to stay in the past. I needed a second chance to make a good life for myself. I should have known that could never be." He paused for a moment and shuffled forward a little. "This is not my first time behind bars. I was jailed as a boy. My father and his friends were all hanged for robbery, but I was just a boy and the judge took pity on me. He sent me to prison."

"Prison?" Marta echoed.

"I was just ten, and I was released just after my eighteenth birthday. I told you that I moved around a lot, well that was why. Nobody wants to hire a man who's been in jail. They don't care why you were there, or that you served your time, or that you were barely old enough to know right from wrong when it all happened. They judge you long before they even consider getting to know you."

His voice was bitter, full of venom for all the times he had been dismissed and made to move on. Marta wanted to reach out to him, to hold him, to let him know that he need not ever fear that again, but it was clear that he did need to fear it. He was living it all over again. "But why do they think you murdered someone?" she asked.

"There was a man who knew all about my past, and he was angry and twisted because he was losing everything he'd worked hard for all his life. He needed someone to blame, so he went to Mr. Hill, the man I was working for, and demanded he run me off his land. I wanted no trouble for Mr. Hill or Nev. They were my friends, and they knew about my past and trusted me anyway. I couldn't betray that trust by bringing Hanley down on them."

"So, you came here?" Marta said, furrowing her brow. "And you did not tell me why?"

He sighed deeply, and his eyes were filled with tears when he looked up at her. "I just wanted to leave all of that behind me. I wanted to tell you, but I couldn't bear the thought of you turning me away. And the more I came to know you, the more I loved you and the less I could bear the thought of telling you anything that might bring you pain. I am so very sorry for that. I should have told you everything from the very start."

"You should have. I would not have judged you for something you did as a boy. Nobody should."

"Yet men do," he said angrily. "And now, somehow, Hanley has framed me for a murder I most certainly did not commit and I can do nothing to change it. He'll get what he has always wanted, my neck hanging from a noose. He wins."

Elias sank down onto the floor, his back against the wall. "Go, Marta. You deserve so much better than me. Forget me."

"And what if I can't?" she asked. "What if I do not want to? You may have given up, Elias Groves, but I have not. And Richard will not. And your friends here will not."

"Let me rot, as I should have done eighteen years ago," he said, his voice full of despair. "I cannot offer you the life you deserve, and I will not have you see me brought down by that wretch of a man. Hanley doesn't deserve to see how much he's taken from me, from you. He just doesn't."

CHAPTER 20

*D*ecember 2, 1890, Santa Fe, New Mexico

Elias had hoped never to see this courtroom ever again. It hadn't changed in eighteen years. It was here that he had promised his father that he would make something of himself, that he would not end up hanging from a noose for all the world to see, and yet here he was, back in the dock, about to be tried for a crime that could only see him on the gallows. He should be afraid, but he was quietly resigned to it. He always had been, he had realized that when Marta had fled from the sheriff's office in Iron Creek, sobbing.

That was at least one good thing. She was not there to see his demise. He had made it clear to Richard, when he'd come and offered his services, that he did not want her to be in New Mexico when his trial happened. He did not want her to see him die, accused and committed for a crime he had most certainly not committed. And then he had told Richard that he did not want him to act as his lawyer, either. He knew that there was no point in fighting the inevitability of this day, and he would not ruin Richard's reputation and drag him down with him.

It didn't matter that Sheriff Hansen said that he believed him when he said that he couldn't have possibly committed the murder as he had been on his way to Minnesota when it took place. It didn't matter that Richard believed him, or that Garrett had said he would support him and do all it took to set him free. All that mattered was that he was back where it had all started, where his father had been sentenced to death, where he had been given a chance to make a better life. If only others in the world could have been as forgiving as the judge that day and as kind as Warden Greenslade had been to him.

But the world was not forgiving. And Uriah Hanley in particular was unforgiving. Elias glanced around the court-room, and sure enough, Hanley was sitting in the very front row of the public gallery, looking fat and smug, as if he alone had been responsible for bringing a dangerous crim-inal to justice. Elias wanted to charge across the room and throttle the man, but that would only prove Hanley's point that Elias was not to be trusted because he had violent urges that made the public unsafe.

Instead, Elias stared at him. As he did so, Hanley seemed

to grow uncomfortable. He started fidgeting in his seat and running a pudgy finger around his collar as if trying to loosen it, and his florid face grew redder. Elias smiled at him, knowing that it would drive the older man crazy to think that he wasn't bothered by everything that was going on around him. It was the best and only revenge that he could take for the way Uriah Hanley had ruined his life.

The door to the gallery opened behind Hanley. Elias was momentarily distracted when he saw the Hills enter and take their seats with a nod of support to him. Moments later, Sheriff Hansen and Mayor Winston entered. He knew the sheriff was in Santa Fe, of course. He'd brought Elias here, after all. But the kindly mayor's presence was unexpected. Mayor Winston gave him a little nod and a small smile of encouragement, and Elias felt his heart soar. Even if he had not gotten the second chance that he had longed for, he had finally found a home and true friends who cared for him. That meant the world to him.

Not needing to play with Uriah Hanley any longer, Elias turned back to face the front of the courtroom and waited for the judge to appear. First, the prosecutor emerged from a room to the side of the court. Elias had no lawyer. He suddenly regretted that and wished that he had taken Richard up on his offer to represent him. He was stunned when Richard appeared just a few minutes later. As the lawyer passed Elias in the dock, he reached up and shook his hand, giving him a wink.

"I knew you didn't mean it," he said with a smile. "And, so that you know, Marta is well. She is staying with Emily at the house. She sends you all her love. She knew you didn't want her to be here but wanted to come anyway. I had to insist that she stay in Iron Creek, and Emily promised that she wouldn't let her out of her sight."

Elias smiled at the thought of the headstrong Marta being foiled in her attempt to travel to Santa Fe to be by his side. But his smile soon became a frown when he thought of how broken she would be when Richard returned home and told her of the inevitable outcome of his trial. It felt so unjust that he should be facing charges for a murder he had not committed, one he could not have committed, all because of one bitter old man's need to show that he still held some sway in New Mexico.

The judge emerged from his chambers and frowned at everyone. A hush settled over the court as he asked Elias to make his plea.

"Not guilty," he responded, loudly and clearly.

And the trial began. Elias was amazed at how much work Richard had done and how effectively he questioned the few witnesses brought forward by the prosecution. Hanley was the most convincing. His testimony that he'd seen Elias near the barn where the man's body had been found sounded plausible. He spoke clearly and seemingly without rancor, but the way his mouth curled into a little sneer every time he looked at Elias made his words hold less weight than they could have done. Unfortunately, his standing in the community made him an effective witness, and there weren't many men who'd gainsay him, even though his ranch was now little more than fifty head of cattle and around a quarter of the land he'd once possessed.

It was then Richard's turn to bring up his witnesses. Somehow, he had managed to find the guard on the train that night, and he remembered Elias well because he'd been the one to alert him to Jet's discomfort.

"I was impressed by a man who gave up the comfort of his seat in the carriages to settle in the cattle cars with his horse," the guard said with nodding approval. "I doubt many men would have done the same."

It was a small detail, but not only did it place Elias over a hundred miles from the place the murder had taken place, it also established that he was a good and kind man, one unlikely to harm an animal, so even more unlikely to harm another man. Elias would be forever grateful to the man for coming and saying what he had, and he finally began to have hope that he might leave the courtroom a free man.

When he saw Richard's next witness, he almost cried. Mayor Winston took the stand and testified to Elias' character. After him, Garrett took the stand. Then Sheriff Hansen did. His testimony was very powerful. He spoke of how he'd received the wanted poster with Elias' picture and how he'd done his job and brought him in, but he also swore that he believed Elias had not done it and would never do such a thing.

Then Mr. Hill and Nev testified. They told the court why Elias had left New Mexico. Mr. Hill spoke calmly of Uriah Hanley's determination to run him out of New Mexico, though Nev was a little more vehement in his opinion of Hanley. Neither said that they thought that Hanley was responsible for bringing Elias back to the state to be put on trial for a murder he could not have committed, but the meaning of their words was clear. Hanley grew more and more uncomfortable as each of them spoke and stormed out of the gallery before Nev had finished speaking. None of Elias' witnesses buckled as the prosecutor barked his questions at them, trying to gainsay them in whatever way he could. Elias was so grateful to each and every one of them that he could have hugged and kissed them all, but he tried to keep his face solemn as he watched the impact each of their testimonies had on the judge and jury.

Then it was time for the jury to go and make their decisions. Elias was taken to a small cell at the rear of the courtroom, and Richard joined him.

"How did you do that?" Elias asked, shaking Richard's hand with grateful exuberance.

"I just listened to what you told me, and what you'd told Matt. Between us, we tracked down the people you spoke of. It's what we do," Richard said with a smile. "Glad you had a lawyer now?"

"I am, and I will spend the rest of my days trying to pay you back for this," Elias admitted. "I should never have pushed everyone away. I've just never had people who were on my side before. I've been moved on and pushed away so often, I just didn't believe anyone would stand by me."

"We know you, Elias. Marta knows you and loves you. And she is waiting for you to come home and marry her. I'll not be able to go home if this goes against us."

Elias noted his use of the word us. It felt wonderful to be part of an "us." He'd always been on his own. But no longer. Now, he was a part of Iron Creek. He had a home and friends, and he prayed that he would soon have a wife and a family of his own – one that would never have to resort to the lengths that his father had done to try to keep food in their bellies. "Do you think I stand a chance?"

"I think that you stand as good a chance as any man I've ever represented. The evidence is in your favor, and Hanley's vendetta against you looked bad. He is the only person who places you within a hundred miles of his ranch. I think he may just find that the finger of suspicion begins to fall on him. It was his land, and there are a lot of rumors that he held a grudge against the dead man. He has a motive, and you do not."

A clerk came to tell Richard that the jury was ready. He shook Elias' hand again. "I'll see you shortly," he said before heading back to the courtroom.

A few minutes later, a sheriff came to lead Elias back

into the courtroom. Hanley was conspicuous by his absence, and Elias wondered if he'd seen the way things were going and gotten as far away from the court, and all the lawmen inside, as he could before they could take him into one of the cells out the back. He was a wily old coot who would have seen the writing on the wall and done all he could to save his own skin.

The judge looked at Elias and gave him a tight smile as he read the verdict of the jury, and then asked them to announce it to the court. The jury foreman stood up and proudly announced Elias "not guilty." Elias felt his knees buckle underneath him and feared he would cry in front of everyone as a surge of emotion flooded through him. The relief was unimaginable. It was an outcome to this dreadful situation that he had never expected. When the judge announced that he was a free man and the sheriff removed the shackles at his wrists, he felt his knees give way and stumbled against the oak barrier. Richard was at his side immediately, offering him a supportive arm around his waist.

"You did it," Elias said, feeling overwhelmed, delighted, and exhausted, all at the same time.

"There was never any question in my mind that we wouldn't," Richard said with a smile as they made their way out of the courtroom. "You simply weren't even close to where the murder occurred, and the only person who could place you there was a man who held a grudge against you and had a motive to kill the victim himself."

"Do you think they will arrest Hanley?"

"If they can find him, I think they might," Richard said.

Mayor Winston, Sheriff Hansen, and the Hills met them at the courtroom doors, and Mr. Hill shook Elias' hand with solemnity.

"That was close, my boy," he said. The old man had tears in his eyes. It was strange to see him so emotional. He'd never seemed the sentimental type to Elias. He suddenly pulled Elias into a bear hug. "I'm so glad Uriah didn't manage to drag you down."

Nev slapped him on the back. "I'm sorry we didn't get to warn you," he said, shaking his head, his face full of chagrin, as if it was their fault that Elias had found himself in front of a judge and jury again. "There was no word locally. No posters went up. We didn't even know that Jeb was missing until it was in the newspaper that you were being brought back for his murder."

"None of this is your fault," Elias assured him.

"We let you down. We promised we'd let you know."

"If you didn't know, how could you have warned me?" Elias said, giving his arm a reassuring squeeze. "But, despite the circumstances, it is good to see you both."

"It is good to see you, too. We got your letter about your wedding. I'm glad it all worked out with your girl," Nev said, punching Elias' arm.

"Right up until I was arrested on my wedding day," Elias said a little bitterly, giving Sheriff Hansen a look.

"I hated doing that," the sheriff said.

"I know you did," Elias said. "And Richard told me you helped him track down all those people who spoke for me, so I am more grateful to you than I can say. I just hope that Marta will be able to forgive me for all the worry I've put her through."

"She loves you," Mayor Winston said softly. "She'll be mad for a while, but she'll have you down the aisle before you know it."

"I pray that you are right," Elias said, but he wasn't as sure as the kindly mayor was. She'd been left behind, on her wedding day. He could not expect her to just accept him back with open arms, but he would do whatever it took to make it up to her.

CHAPTER 21

*D*ecember 3, 1890, Iron Creek, Minnesota

The only thing that had helped Marta get through the weeks of waiting had been her work. Emily, Katy, and everyone else in Iron Creek had been very kind, but their looks of pity and expressions of concern had only served to make her more nervous for Elias. Kneading the dough and creating new pastries while Gertie served their customers in the shop had been a needed distraction. Yesterday had been the hardest day, knowing that Elias was standing in front of a courtroom without her there to support him had driven her half mad with worry.

She should have ignored him and gone to be by his side. He needed to know that she stood by him. She couldn't bear the thought that she might have somehow added to his concerns, that he might have been worried that she no longer loved him or trusted him. She did trust him, implicitly. He had concealed things about his past, she could obviously not deny that he had done that, but he had not lied about them. He had never claimed to be an angel.

Everything that he had concealed had happened so long ago, and he had not even been responsible for his role in his father's criminal past. He had been just a boy. As a man, he simply wanted to leave his past in the past, where it belonged. The man she knew would not hurt a soul. He would not steal so much as a bread roll. He'd insisted on paying her for everything she had ever offered him to try.

But it was almost three o'clock and there was still no news of how the trial had gone. Richard had promised her that he would send a telegram as soon as it was over, and that meant that the trial must have taken longer than a day. That was rare. That he had even had a trial with a judge and jury had been unusual, brought about mainly because of Richard's advocacy. In most situations, such hearings were held before a local magistrate and were often over in mere minutes – and depended entirely upon who the magistrate held in the highest regard. Had Elias been subjected to such a trial, he would no doubt be awaiting a sentence of death now.

Slowly, she began to clean down the kitchen, knowing Gertie would be doing the same out in the shop. The methodical process usually calmed her and helped her to sort out her thoughts, but nothing had helped her in the days since Elias had been taken from her. The reliability of baking, the order of cleaning, and even the comfort of being with Emily had not helped. Every moment, she waited for the clang of the door and prayed that Hank Wilson would burst in with a telegram for her with news of how things were going. Yet nothing came.

When their chores were complete, she and Gertie closed the bakery. It had been snowing off and on for the past week, and it was still bitterly cold. The road was a little treacherous with thick ice where the snow had melted and refrozen, and there was dark slush where wagons and carriages had passed along the street. Marta pulled her fur coat tightly around her and shivered a little. Gertie grinned at her and gave her a hug.

"You'll hear from him soon enough. My Mom always says that no news is good news, so we must hold tight to that thought."

"You're a good girl, Gertie," Marta said. "Go home, get yourself in the warm, and get some rest. I shall see you in the morning."

Marta crossed the street and let herself into Mayor Winston's grand home. The house seemed cold and empty without the kindly mayor in residence, no lights lit, and no fires blazing in the hearths, but she was glad that he had gone to Santa Fe to support Elias. He needed all the friendly faces around him that he could have. Knowing that the mayor was there helped soothe her mind a little, and Richard would not leave any stone unturned in getting to the truth of the matter, she was sure of that. Elias had the best help that she could send him, except herself.

After she had lit a fire in the drawing room, she sank down in a chair in front of it. Emily would stop by after her shift at the clinic, no doubt, and she would insist that Marta go home with her. She'd done so in the early days, immediately after her ill-fated wedding, but she had come to prefer being alone with her fears as time had passed. They had tried so hard to cheer her up and reassure her that all would be well, but there was nothing anyone could do to distract her from the realities that faced poor Elias, and she hated to bring everyone's mood down along with her own.

She closed her eyes. A picture of Elias swam into her imagination, his handsome, kind face looking sad and scared. He had been so ashamed. She knew that he regretted not telling her sooner about his past. He had told her everything from inside his cell in the sheriff's office, tears flooding down his cheeks, full of guilt. He had been so sure that this was the end, and his hopelessness had infected her a little, making her dwell on the worst outcomes far more than the thought that he was innocent. She knew that far too many innocent men, women, and children faced the full force of the law.

Innocence guaranteed nothing. Because of that dark fact, she had barely slept, barely eaten, and been on edge for too long. It was taking its toll. She'd had to take in all of her dresses as the weight fell off her. Her skin was pale and sallow, and there were heavy dark rings under her eyes red from crying. She sighed, wishing there was more she could do. But all that was left to her was to wait, try to be as patient as possible, and then be as stoic as she could if the news that Elias had feared came. She would not let him down.

Marta tried to focus on her breathing and not her thoughts. She was so tired that she was soon dozing in the chair. A loud rapping on the door awoke her with a start. It was dark outside, and she was surprised to see that it was already past six o'clock when she glanced at the clock.

"Miss Pauling, there's a telegram," Mr. Wilson's voice yelled through the closed door. "Come quickly. There's news. There's news."

She jumped out of her chair and ran to the front door. Mr. Wilson was out of breath, his face red from running. She smiled. He looked as happy as he had been on the day he'd brought news that Elias was coming to Iron Creek.

"Is it good news?" she demanded, taking the telegram he held out to her and ripping it open. She knew that, as the operator, he knew what was in every telegram that arrived.

"Oh, it is the very best news," he said, beaming.

She tried to make out the words, but the house was too dark. She lit the lamp on the hallway table, then read the message, her heart racing. Her hands were shaking, and she felt as weak as a kitten.

"Oh, my," she exclaimed when she had finally taken in the words and what they meant. "He's free, and they're on their way home." She leaned against the wall, not sure that her legs were strong enough to carry her.

"They are, and they should be here in time for Christmas," Mr. Wilson said happily. "If they take the swiftest route they can."

"Oh, what a wonderful gift that would be," Marta said, tears pouring down her cheeks. "Thank you, Mr. Wilson, I cannot tell you how happy I am to receive this."

The portly postmaster smiled at her. "My dear, this sort of thing is precisely why I love my job so. Bringing good news, bringing joy. It is a real honor." He paused and peered into the dark and empty house. "Is there someone I could fetch for you? You could use some company, I don't doubt."

"Emily is probably at the clinic," Marta said. "She will be glad to know her husband will be coming home, too, I should imagine."

"I shall send her to you." He nodded and disappeared into the dark street, his feet crunching loudly in the crisp snow underfoot.

Marta knew that it would not take long for the rest of the town to learn the news. Hank Wilson was a terrible gossip, but that was sometimes a good thing. It meant that she would not need to tell everyone. She could simply think about making things perfect for when Elias returned. With a surge of energy she'd not felt in too long, she began thinking about dressing the house for Christmas and the food she would prepare for a great feast for everyone. There was still time to make everything ready, even though she would usually have started making her plans weeks before.

Emily arrived just a few minutes later. She hugged Marta tightly. "They're coming home," she said through happy tears. "I have missed Richard so terribly. Hopefully, you will be able to get a good night's sleep and start to feed yourself again now. Don't think I haven't noticed that you are rail-slat thin these days."

"I'll be as plump as a partridge in no time," Marta assured her. "I want to have a grand banquet on Christmas Eve if they are all back in time. To welcome Elias home and to thank everyone else for all they've done for him. Will you help me with it?"

"Of course. I think it is a wonderful idea. We could have it here. I'm sure Dad would not mind."

"I was thinking somewhere a little larger," Marta said with a smile. "So that we can invite all our friends. Do you think it would be presumptuous if I ask Father Paul to be ready to marry us as soon as Elias returns? I cannot bear the thought that we have lost all this time when we could already have been wed."

Emily grinned. "I cannot tell you how happy I am to have my loving, romantic friend back again. I feared I had lost you. I think that would be wonderful. And I do not doubt that Elias will be delighted to become your husband the very moment he steps off the train."

"Oh, I do hope so," Marta said.

The two friends went into the kitchen and began pulling out dried fruits, flour, suet, butter, sugar, and lots of bowls. Emily followed Marta's direction as they made plum puddings and fruit cakes for the entire town.

"Can you fetch your father's brandy?" Marta asked her as they finished stirring the mix for the puddings. "And his rum for the cakes."

"Of course. I'm sure he will be delighted to know that they were used for such a good cause," Emily said with a grin.

It was past ten o'clock before all the puddings had been tied in their cloths ready to be steamed in the vast pans Marta had at the bakery, and the cakes were in their molds ready to go into the ovens the next morning. Marta yawned loudly and stretched. She took off her apron and laid it over the back of one of the chairs around the big kitchen table. "You know, I think I might actually sleep tonight."

"You deserve to," Emily said. "Do you mind if I stay here tonight? It is too cold out to go back to the house now."

"Of course, but won't Mrs. Ball worry if you don't get home soon?"

"I warned her that I would stay here with you if news came from New Mexico, and I asked Hank to send Thomas out to her when he fetched me from the clinic. She knows that all is well."

"Thank you," Marta said softly. "I bless the day that we became friends."

"I do, too," Emily agreed.

Emily went into the drawing room and banked the fire there while Marta tidied around a little and put enough wood in the stove to keep it warm until the morning. It was horrible to wake up to an ice-cold house when you had to get to work so very early. The warm stove also helped to heat the bedrooms above a little without the risk of having a fire burning unchecked in the bedrooms overnight. The two young women linked arms and went upstairs to bed. They were on the landing before Marta remembered that there was no bed made up in Emily's room.

"It'll take us only a few minutes," she said as she opened the doors of the linen closet.

"Or we could share?" Emily said with a smile. "It's cold, and we're both tired."

Marta nodded. In her bedroom, she pulled a clean nightgown out of the trunk at the end of her bed and threw it to Emily, then took her own out from under the pillow. They changed quickly and scrambled under the covers, Emily with her head at the foot of the bed. Marta threw her a pillow, and they both lay down and pulled the blanket up tight around them. Within moments, Marta was asleep.

CHAPTER 22

*D*ecember 24, 1890, Iron Creek, Minnesota

As the early afternoon train was drawing close to Iron Creek, all five men were excited to be almost home. They had feared that they might be delayed along their route, but they had thankfully made every train change on time. Richard and Sheriff Hansen longed to see their wives, Mayor Winston was looking forward to being home and seeing Mrs. Ball and Emily, and Elias was both happy and nervous all at once. His last meeting with Marta had been hard on them both. He had been so sure that she would reject him for his lies, and she had been rightfully angry with him for not telling her.

But she had also been supportive of him – something he had not expected and felt he had no right to. He knew that it was thanks to her that Richard had come to Santa Fe. He knew that it was down to her that Richard and Sheriff Hansen had worked so hard to find the evidence needed to prove he was innocent. And he knew that she had done all she could to make sure that people who cared about him had been present even though he had asked her not to be.

Seeing faces that he knew and loved in that courtroom had buoyed his spirits, but he was glad she had heeded his words and not come herself. Sheriff Hansen hadn't had him in shackles, but he had not been allowed out of them once he'd been handed over to the sheriffs in Santa Fe. He'd have hated for Marta to see him that way.

He was also afraid. Just because she had done all she could for him did not mean that she would still want to become his wife. There had been many weeks for her to think upon the folly of marrying a man like him. He would accept her decision if she no longer wanted to be wed, but it would break his heart into a million pieces. All he wanted was for her to be happy, and if he could not bring her happiness, he prayed that there was someone who could.

The train's whistle sounded, alerting the guard at the station in Iron Creek that their arrival was imminent. Elias' belly was full of writhing snakes. In just a few minutes, he would find out if Marta still cared for him, if she could forgive him for his past and for not telling her about it. He couldn't bear the thought that she might reject him. If she did, he would have to move on again, leaving the place he had come to think of as his home forever. Much as he wanted her to be happy, he knew he would not be able to bear seeing her with another man.

When the train began to slow, Sheriff Hansen stood up and reached up to the rack above their heads for his bag. He took it down and placed it on the seat before reaching for Mayor Winston's. The older man smiled.

"Thank you, Matt," he said. He pulled on his coat, then took a thick scarf out of his bag and wrapped it around his throat.

Richard also stood up and reached for his bag, then threw Garrett's down to him. Garrett caught it and grinned.

"I cannot wait to see my wife," Garrett said with a soft whistle. "I haven't been apart from her for so long since we were married. I've even missed the children." Everyone laughed; they all knew just how devoted a father Garrett was to his seemingly ever-increasing brood.

Richard handed Elias the small carpet bag Garrett had brought with a couple of changes of clothes in it. Elias hugged it tightly against his chest. His breathing was suddenly very shallow, and his hands were shaking.

"She'll be glad to see you," Richard assured him. "She loves you."

"She *loved* me," Elias corrected. "She's had a lot of time to change her mind, and good reason to do so."

"Marta is not a girl to be swayed," Richard said with a grin. "She knows her own mind. She'll be there on the platform, waiting for you. I know it."

Elias prayed he was right, but he also knew that Christmas Eve was a busy day in the bakery. Marta had told him how hard it was in the week before Christmas, ensuring everyone had everything they needed for a feast on Christmas Day, but he had gotten the impression that she rather enjoyed being busy and being able to sneak a few treats into the baskets of those in town who had less than others so they too could enjoy a wondrous Christmas. She had such a kind heart.

He had no doubts in his mind that Emily would be there to greet her father and husband, and Katy would no doubt bring the children down the mountain in the wagon to greet Garrett. Mrs. Hansen might not be there – she was possibly used to her husband being away for a time, taking fugitives to wherever they needed to face justice – but just looking at the sheriff's face told him that he hoped she would be there to meet them.

When the train came to a halt, Elias peered out of the window, trying to see if anyone was waiting for them. He couldn't see much through the fog of smoke and steam that filled the platform briefly. But when he could, his heart lifted. Marta was standing with Emily, their arms linked, her eyes straining to see into all of the carriages, looking for him. He didn't dare believe that all was well. He knew that he had a lot to do to make up for the strain he had put her through, but she was there, and that meant there was hope that she would let him do so.

As Richard leaned out of the window and opened their door, Sheriff Hansen looked at Elias and held out his hand. "I am sorry I had to put you through all that," he said. "Sometimes, I hate my job."

"I understood that from the start, Sheriff Hansen," Elias assured him. "Thank you for having faith in me, and for helping Richard to prove my innocence. I don't think I'll ever be able to repay either of you for that."

"Let's just say we're even," the sheriff said with a smile. "And it is Matt. After all we've gone through, I hope that we can say we are now friends."

"I'd like that, though I never thought such a thing would ever be possible," Elias said with a wry chuckle. "Me, friends with a sheriff."

They all laughed. Richard jumped down from the train and offered Mayor Winston a hand. The older man had quite short legs, and the distance from the step of the train to the platform was quite large. In moments, Emily was in Richard's arms, then being hugged tightly by her father. Elias smiled when he saw Clara Hansen hugging her husband, then him picking up their young children and hugging them tightly and smothering their faces with kisses. Garrett kissed his wife passionately, then herded his children out of the station with a wave to the others as he went.

Marta had stayed back from the platform edge, watching as everyone else hugged and kissed one another. Elias had waited by the train door. They looked at each other awkwardly. Marta looked a little thin and very tired. He bit his lip, knowing he must have caused her so much hurt, so much worry. Then suddenly, she rushed forward and enveloped him in her arms.

"I am so glad you are home safe," she said, her bright blue eyes full of tears. "I have been so scared for you."

"I was a little concerned for the outcome, myself," Elias admitted. "But I was even more worried that you would hate me."

"Why ever would I hate you?" she asked, looking utterly perplexed by such an idea.

"Because I lied to you. Because of all of this."

"Pshaw," she said dismissively. "You might have omitted to tell me what happened to you as a boy, but I did not know that boy. I do know the man in front of me, and I know that he is good and honest and would not ever harm a living soul. So, no, I do not hate you. I hope that we will have no secrets between us in the future, that you know you can tell me anything. I love you. I am not here to judge you. I am happy to leave that to God."

"You love me?" Elias echoed.

"Yes, I do. Very much," she said with a soft smile.

"Oh, thank the very heavens above for that." He sighed, bent his head to her uptilted face, and kissed her lips. They were warm and soft, and he longed to kiss her forever.

They were interrupted by Emily, who flung her arms around him in a huge hug once he'd finally let Marta go.

"We have been in bits," she told him as they all made their way out of the station. "Marta wasn't sleeping or eating. But when we got that telegram, it was like a miracle."

"It felt like one when the jury said I was innocent," Elias said, grinning at her.

"It seems the snow has finally come," Mayor Winston said, noting the thick snow on the ground and the icicles hanging from the roofs of most of the buildings along Main Street.

"It has been bitterly cold," Marta said. She looked at Elias and his thin coat. "You never did go to see Old Porter, did you?"

"No," he admitted. "I rather thought I had a little more time. I shall go and see him after Christmas."

"You wait until you see what we've been doing," Emily bubbled happily. "I do so hope none of you are too tired to enjoy it after your long travels."

Richard raised a quizzical eyebrow. "What have you two been up to?"

"Nothing much," Marta said, glaring at Emily a little as if she'd given away a secret she wasn't supposed to.

"There's no big secret. We've just been decorating the house for Christmas and preparing for a family meal tomorrow," Emily said after a brief and awkward pause. She gave Marta an apologetic look that suggested there might be more to it than that, but only Elias seemed to have noticed it. He began to wonder if he'd imagined the tension between them in that brief moment, and as they drew close to the house and he saw the large holly wreath on the door, with lots of bright red berries poking out from the dark green foliage, he stopped thinking about it.

When they entered the house, it became clear that they really had been busy. Every surface was decorated with boughs of evergreens. The greenery even twined around the spindles of the banister. And everywhere smelled of pine and cinnamon.

"Something smells delicious," Mayor Winston said. He took off his coat and scarf and followed his nose to his kitchen. Mrs. Ball was standing at the stove, stirring a large pot of mulled cider, and there was a rich fruit cake on the table. He licked his lips, picked up a knife, and started cutting it into pieces. Once they'd all taken off their coats and hung them up and Emily had poured them all a cup of the warming cider, he handed everyone a slice and they all sat down around the big kitchen table.

"So glad to have you all home," Mrs. Ball said. She hugged her nephew, then kissed Mayor Winston's flushed cheek.

"Poor Elias had a torrid time, but he's home now," Mayor Winston said. "And will be for a very long time, I do hope."

"I have no intention of moving on anywhere as long as Marta wants me to be here," Elias said, taking Marta's hand and squeezing it gently.

"So, will you be arranging your wedding soon?" Mrs. Ball asked. Again, Emily and Marta shared a peculiar look. And again, they composed themselves quickly. This time, it seemed that Richard had seen it, too. He gave his wife a quizzical look. Elias knew they were up to something but had no idea what.

"If Marta will still have me as her husband, I hope that we will be able to marry early in the New Year," he said. "But she is under no obligation to do so if she has changed her mind."

"I've not changed my mind," she assured him, squeezing his hand tightly. "I'd marry you this minute if I could."

"I'm glad to hear that," Emily announced. "Now, I think that we should all get some rest. You've all had a long journey and must want to get cleaned up and have a nap. Perhaps we can all dine together this evening?"

"I'd like that," Mayor Winston said.

Elias was exhausted, but he would much rather have spent a few hours with Marta now and made his way back up to the bunkhouse for a little peace and quiet and a good night's sleep. There were things they needed to talk about. He needed to be sure that she truly was happy to continue their engagement and that she truly understood and forgave him for not telling her. But it seemed that such a talk would have to wait because Marta looked so eager at the thought of a big meal together. Mrs. Ball retired to the room that had been made up for her when she and Richard had stayed there after her attack of apoplexy before Richard and Emily had married, and Emily and Richard made their way up to her old room. Marta took him up to a bright and clean bedroom overlooking Main Street.

"Will this be comfortable enough?" she asked, glancing around a little nervously.

"Marta, it is perfect. After all that time in jail and on a train, I'd be glad of a scrap of floor with some straw on it."

"Well, this is slightly more comfortable than that," she said. She stood on tiptoe and kissed his cheek. "Get some rest. We've all the time in the world for you to tell me about it and how terrible it must have been."

"Don't let me sleep too long," he said. "I'd not want to be late for this *dinner.*" He stressed the final word, letting her know that he knew something was going on.

She just grinned at him. "I'll send up the bath for you. You'll want to be very clean for it."

CHAPTER 23

*D*ecember 24, 1890, Iron Creek, Minnesota

The house was quiet, though the peace was occasionally punctuated by one of Mayor Winston's rumbling snores. "He's rolled over again," Emily said each time it happened, and the girls laughed about it as they took their baths in front of the fire. Marta tapped her fingers nervously on the top of the dressing table and tried not to let her thoughts run away with her as she waited for Emily to finish. What if she had judged this all wrong? What if the thing Elias had wanted to talk to her about earlier was that he needed a little time?

Emily eased her body out of the tub and wrapped herself in a large bath sheet before pulling on her undergarments and a robe. She picked up Marta's vanity set of two brushes, an ivory hand mirror, and some pins and placed it on the bed, then gestured for Marta to sit in front of her.

"You must be so happy that he is home, free, and innocent," Emily said as she carefully plaited Marta's hair into tiny braids.

"I cannot tell you how much," Marta said. "You must have missed Richard dreadfully, too."

"Of course I did, but I always had the reassurance that he would be returning, even though Elias' life did hang in the balance."

"It did, but I trusted that Elias could not have done such a thing. And I grew ever more convinced with everything Richard and Sheriff Hansen found out."

"Did you not worry that it might not go Elias' way even with all that? I'm not sure that I could have been so confident in the effectiveness of the courts," Emily said thoughtfully. "For the rich, there is always the justice they wish for, but for a humble man like Elias, one who has already been in trouble, well, it isn't always so straightforward."

"I know that," Marta said, "but I had to convince myself that it would all work out. The alternative was to dwell on the very worst that could happen, and I couldn't bear the thought that Elias might be killed for a crime he did not commit."

Emily gave her a quick hug. "I still can't believe you're going to spring a surprise wedding on him," she said as she returned to fixing Marta's hair. "It is so bold, but I don't blame you one bit for doing so."

"I simply will not waste another day," Marta said firmly. "I want to be his wife, and he said that he still wants me to be his wife. Can you blame me for wanting it to happen swiftly? We should already have been married for almost two months. I feel we have been robbed of precious time together."

"I understand entirely," Emily said, starting to pin the delicate braids into tiny swirls. "I was so ready to be Richard's wife."

Emily hummed a little as she continued her work. Marta had said that she did not need anything too fancy, but Emily had insisted, and it had turned out to be a good thing as it filled the time until that evening well. When she was finally finished, she handed Marta a small ivory looking glass. Marta gasped. Her hair looked as lovely as that of any of the fancy ladies she and Emily had so enjoyed watching on the streets of Boston in the days before they had moved to Iron Creek.

"I love it!" she exclaimed, taking another look in the mirror. The line of her jaw and the length of her neck were all enhanced by the way Emily had pinned her hair. She did not look like herself; she looked like an elegant young lady about to start the very next chapter of her life.

"Now, let us get you dressed and out of the house before

Elias awakes," Emily said with a smile. "We don't want him to see your gown, even though he's already seen you today."

"We did everything right last time," Marta said sadly. "It didn't bring us much luck then. I'm rather hoping that we'll make our own luck rather than holding with silly superstitions."

"Then you don't want my pendant for your something borrowed and something blue?" Emily teased, holding out a gorgeous sapphire necklace that Richard had bought for her birthday.

"You are willing to lend that to me?" Marta said, taking it in her hands. It was such a beautiful setting, and such jewels were things that she and Emily could have only dreamed of owning in the past.

"I am," Emily said, beaming at Marta's response to her surprise. "It will match your dress and your lovely eyes perfectly."

Marta's wedding dress was the one she and Emily had made for her aborted wedding. Marta had thought of having a new one made, given all that had gone wrong before, but she so loved it and longed to be able to wear it for Elias, as she had originally planned to. It was cornflower blue, the same shade as her eyes, with an embroidered bodice and flowing skirt that trailed slightly behind her as she walked. Emily helped her into it and carefully fastened every single one of the more than twenty seed pearl buttons at the back.

"You look perfect," Emily said with a sigh. "Even more so than before."

Marta turned to look at herself in the full-length cheval glass. Emily was right. She did look lovely. "He will be happy I've done this, won't he?" she asked, turning back to her friend as a sudden pang of anxiety struck.

"He will be delighted," Emily said. "He loves you, and I'm sure he feels the same way as you do, that you have been robbed of enough time together already."

"But he talked about being wed in the New Year. Perhaps he'd rather wait a little? Perhaps he needs a little time to get over all that has happened to him?"

"Stop fretting. All will be well. Now, let me get dressed, we'll call on Aunt Mary, and then we shall all make our way to the town hall. You can calm your nerves by checking that the buffet is prepared and laid out to your liking."

ELIAS WOKE to the sound of a gentle rapping on the door. He sat up and rubbed his eyes. "Come in," he called. A young girl and a young lad carried in a copper tub and placed it in front of the fireplace. The bath that Marta had promised him. Elias smiled as they disappeared without a word then returned moments later with buckets full of piping hot water. They filled the tub and left him a bath sheet, soap, and a cloth to wash with, then closed the door behind them as they left.

Elias stretched and got out of bed. He took off his underclothes and got into the hot bath. He'd not felt truly clean since he'd left Iron Creek. The lingering stench of the jail had stayed in his nostrils, and on his skin, a constant reminder of where he had been for the past couple of months, no matter how well he'd tried to wash during the journey home. He took the soap and began to scrub his body so hard that his skin began to redden. He wanted to scrub the past weeks off his body, out of his head. He hadn't admitted to anyone just how afraid he had been that he would meet the same end as his feckless father. But the fear had its own stink, and he feared that he might never be able to rid his senses of that. He washed his hair, rubbing hard at his scalp, dunked his head into the water to rinse off the suds, then lathered it again, and again, and again.

The water was cold by the time he accepted that the smell could only be in his head by now. Wearily, he got out of the tub and dried himself off. He frowned when he saw that his clothes were missing, but then noticed a fancy suit hanging on the door of the armoire. He looked a little closer and realized that it was the suit that Garrett had insisted he buy to get married in. On the chair by the bed was a clean shirt and some underclothes. He got dressed quickly and combed his hair. Apparently, this dinner was to be a fancy one if he needed to be so well dressed for it.

Slowly, he made his way downstairs, expecting to see the large table in the dining room set for the fancy meal ahead, but there was not so much as a teaspoon upon it. He heard the sound of clinking glass in the study and headed toward it. Richard and Mayor Winston were there, drinking brandy.

"Would you like one, before we go?" the mayor asked him.

"I wouldn't say no," Elias admitted. "But I thought we were to dine here? Where is it that we are going?"

"Just to the town hall. Marta invited a few of your friends. Many people have been looking forward to your return. She thought it might be nice for them to join us tonight as well."

"And she is already there?"

"Of course. She and Emily left about half an hour ago. They wanted to ensure that everything is just the way Marta wants it. She is quite the stickler when it comes to how her food is."

"She is, which is why she is so good at it," Elias agreed.

"You look much better," Richard said as Mayor Winston poured another glass of brandy and handed it to Elias.

"A good rest and a bath does wonders," Elias said. "I am so tired I could sleep for a week, but I am very much looking forward to some of Marta's fine cooking before I do so."

"She has been preparing for weeks," Mayor Winston said. "The house has never smelt so delicious in all my years here."

There was a pile of beautifully wrapped gifts in the corner of the room. Richard took one from the top of the pile. "Now, it is not Christmas until tomorrow, but Marta told me to make sure that you got to open this before we leave the house tonight." He handed it to Elias.

The parcel was bulky and a little squishy. Elias untied the pretty red bow around it and folded back the paper. He grinned. Inside was a beautiful fur coat. He shook it out and put it on.

"It fits perfectly," Mayor Winston noted. "I'm so glad. We were both so worried we'd not get the size right."

"One of Old Porter's, I presume?" Elias said, as the warmth of the thick pelt began to seep into his bones.

"Of course. Nobody hunts or prepares finer skins in the state," Richard said, admiring the coat.

"Shall we go?" Mayor Winston asked.

He and Richard pulled on their own coats, and the three men walked to the new town hall. It was a large, well-built cabin. Light spilled onto the snowy ground outside, making it look warm and inviting. Elias could hear lots of people talking loudly as they drew closer. It seemed that half the town had turned out for Marta's welcome home meal, not just a few close friends. He smiled, touched by the effort that she had gone to on his behalf and happy that so many people wanted to welcome him home.

Mayor Winston opened the doors, and they went inside. A large fire crackled in a vast hearth at the other end of the hall. In the crowd, Elias could see the Hardings, the Jenks, Dirk and Paul, Zaaga and Dibikad, Sheriff Hansen and his wife, Clara, and many more familiar faces. But the one that drew him, as always, was the face of the woman he adored. Marta looked radiant, clad in a beautiful blue gown, her hair pinned in elaborate whirls. She looked stunning and his breath caught at the sight of her.

She floated toward him as if she was walking on air. "Welcome home," she said before kissing him on the lips. "I hope you like your Christmas present. It certainly fits you well."

He grinned. "I love it and cannot thank you enough. The air is bitingly cold out there tonight. I was most glad of its warmth."

"I'm glad. I couldn't have my fiancé wandering around like an ice block."

"You've gone to a lot of trouble," he said, noticing a long table down one side of the hall, filled with delicious-looking treats. "I'm not worth it."

"You are to me, and to everyone here," she said. "Everyone missed you and prayed for you. You might not realize it, but you are much loved here." She stopped, suddenly looking a little nervous. She started to wring her hands and seemed to be struggling to find the words she wanted to say.

Elias took her arms in his hands "What is it? There is

nothing you cannot say to me, I hope. And we did promise no more secrets, did we not?"

She gave him a wry smile. "Well, you see," she said awkwardly. She stopped and shook her head. "Well, I did all this and invited all these people because I, well, I rather wondered if perhaps you might like to marry me?"

CHAPTER 24

*D*ecember 24, 1890, Iron Creek Minnesota

"Of course I want to marry you," Elias said, a little puzzled by her question. He'd surely already told her earlier that he wanted them to be wed.

"I meant now," she said with a shy smile. "Will you marry me here, tonight?"

"Tonight?" he asked. "But surely that isn't possible? There's no priest, and I doubt he'd have time, what with all the Christmas services and things ahead for him."

"Well, he's waiting in the church for us now," Marta said. "If you really do still want to marry me, I don't want to wait until the New Year. We've already lost so much time together."

"Come outside with me for a moment," Elias said,

feeling suddenly overwhelmed. He was delighted that Marta wanted to marry him as soon as possible, but some questions needed to be asked. He hadn't just been away for work; he'd been in jail cells, in the custody of a sheriff. And she knew nothing about his past except the barest details. How could she be sure that she wanted to marry him?

She let him guide her outside even though she wasn't wearing a coat. Immediately, he took his off and put it around her shoulders.

"What is wrong?" she asked him, her blue eyes searching his.

"Nothing and everything," he said. He bit his lip. "Marta, we need to talk about everything that has happened. I cannot marry you until I am sure that you truly know who it is that you are marrying."

"Elias, I have told you before. You are not the boy who did as his father told him and was punished for other men's crimes. You are not the man who was run off ranches when the drive was over because nobody wanted a ranch hand who had been in jail. You are not even the man who was arrested two months ago, who was so afraid that he would end up like his father that he wanted to push everyone who cares about him away at the very time he needed them the most."

"Marta…" He stopped speaking when she glared at him.

"Have you stopped loving me?" she demanded.

"Of course not," he assured her hurriedly. "I adore you, but you deserve so much more than me. I am not a good man."

"There are more than forty people in that room." Marta pointed back at the hall. "Every single one of them knows that you are a good man. Perhaps we all know you better than you know yourself. How many times do you need to hear that you are not your past? You are all the things you have learned from your past. You have had some big lessons, and you chose to be a good, law-abiding man. It is not your fault that so many in your life before were not prepared to see that."

"Marta, I know you think you know…" She stared at him, anger flashing in her eyes, so he stopped what he had been about to say. "Marta, I still stink of jail. I'm not sure if the stench will ever leave me. I truly believed that my life was done. That changes a man. I'm not sure if I will ever be able to live a life without fear that such a thing might happen again."

"Is there anyone else out there holding a mortal grudge?" Marta asked him, quite calmly.

"Not as far as I am aware, but that doesn't mean that there isn't someone."

"I understand why you are wary. I understand that your trust is hard-earned, and that it is hard for you to bring your-self to believe that you deserve a good life, but you do.

There are people here who not only trust you but also truly care for you. Garrett, Dirk, Paul, Mayor Winston, Richard, Dibikad. Everyone who meets you finds you charming, kind, and generous to a fault. Mrs. Cable told me all about the time that you carried her shopping home from the market because she was feeling a little under the weather, and Nelly thinks you are just wonderful because you are so polite and always doff your hat when you see her." She paused and took his face between her palms. "And I love you. I know everything that you think should make me turn away, but none of that matters to me because none of that changes who you are today. The man I love. The man who makes me laugh. The man who made me long to meet him from his very first letter. And I want to marry you. I have no doubts in my mind whatsoever. But now is the time to say if you do or if you don't love me and want to be with me."

Elias could hardly believe his ears. All his life, he had longed to be accepted. He hadn't ever hoped for much more than that, and even such a small thing had often seemed unattainable. Yet here he was, standing in front of the woman he loved with all his heart, and she was telling him that he was accepted, and loved, here in Iron Creek. That he had friends and a home. And her. And he was making her feel that he had reservations about being her husband.

"Marta, I love you with all my heart. I cannot express just how much I want to be married to you. But you must understand my concern for you. I do not want you to do something in haste that you come to regret."

"My only regret is that we are not already wed," she said stubbornly. "So, I am going to make my way to the church. If you and all our guests join me there in ten minutes, I shall be the happiest woman alive. If you do not, I understand that, too, and we will wait until you are sure that I know my own mind."

She took the coat off her shoulders and handed it to him before walking along the street to the church. Elias realized that she must have been freezing, but she did not even wrap her arms around herself to keep warm. She just strode purposefully, her shoulders straight and her head high.

A part of him wanted to laugh at how ridiculous all of this was. Why was he fighting the thing he wanted most in the world? She seemed utterly sure of what she wanted. He was completely sure that he wanted it, too. Yet they were arguing about it. He shook his head and pulled on the coat as he began to shiver quite violently. He took a few steps toward the door of the hall, then stopped. With his hand still on the door handle, he wondered what he would say when he went inside. Before he had decided, the door pushed back toward him. Elias jumped back out of the way. Garrett gave him a searching look.

"Is everything alright between the two of you?" he asked, clearly concerned.

"I'm not sure," Elias said. "She wants to marry me. Tonight."

"And you aren't happy about that?"

"I should be."

"But you have doubts?" Garrett asked. Elias nodded. "I'd like to think that the two of us know each other well, and I class you as a friend and not just a cowboy who works for me. So, as a friend, I am going to reassure you that there are many men in this town with far shadier pasts than yours. You were a boy. You did as your father told you to. You were punished harshly, and you have told yourself that you are no good ever since. You believed that you would hang because you thought the jury would see the man you see in yourself."

Elias bristled a little at the harshness of Garrett's summary, but he knew he was right. Marta was right. He was his own worst enemy, not Uriah Hanley or the judge who had sent him to jail as a boy, not even his father. Garrett put a hand on his shoulder and shook his head.

"Elias, you are a hardworking, decent man. You know more about cows than any man should ever have to, and you are good with my children. They adore you, and you always have time to play with them no matter how busy you are. It is time to recognize that man that loves Marta and who deserves a wonderful life with her."

"I don't know how to," Elias admitted.

"Just keep doing what comes naturally to you. The

change in perspective will come in time. Believe me, I see myself in a totally different light than the way I did before I met Katy. Marta will get you there. Trust in that." He grinned. "Now, shall I go and fetch everyone for a trip to the church, or are you skipping town again? Because if you hurt her, there are few folk in town who'll forgive you for it. It'll put her off her baking!"

"We go to the church," Elias said softly. "We go to the church."

"Good man."

Marta was waiting in the vestry, her head in her hands, praying silently that she would soon hear footsteps in the church. Father Paul gave her a sad smile. "He'll come," he assured her. "Elias is not a fool, and you did rather spring this all upon him."

"I fear he might be a fool," Marta said bitterly. "He's being so stubborn and silly."

"Ah, men can get in their own way at times," the priest assured her. "But we get it right in the end."

The sound of boots clattering on the flagstones alerted them to the presence of someone in the church. "I'll just go and see who is there," Father Paul said, laying a warm hand on her shoulder as he walked past her. It was as comforting as if he had laid a blessing upon her. Marta prayed that whoever was outside had not come to tell her that there would be no wedding. For all Elias' silliness, she loved him. She knew that he was not what he believed himself to be, and she would happily spend her lifetime convincing him of that – if he would just let her.

Father Paul came back into the vestry at a run. "He's here. We're going to have a wedding, Marta, my dear."

Marta felt tears begin to fall down her cheeks. He had seen sense. She was so relieved, but she was still angry at him for putting her through such torment. Not far behind Father Paul, Emily hurried into the vestry. She took one look at Marta and frowned.

"Sit still," she said, hastily taking out some of the pins in Marta's hair. "You've managed to pull half your hair out." She carefully tucked the stray strands where they should be and then pinned them again. "Better, but there's not much I can do about the red eyes."

"Father Paul, do you have some water I can splash my face with?" Marta asked.

"Only in the font," he said. "Wait just a moment, I shall fetch you some."

"He'll be needing that again soon," Emily said with a grin. "I've not told Richard yet. I was going to do so tomorrow, as a Christmas gift. Today is all about you and Elias, so not a word, but Dr. Anna confirmed it this morning. We're going to have a baby, and it should be with us in August."

Marta jumped up and hugged her friend tightly. "Oh, that

is the most wonderful news. I promise not to tell a soul until you've told Richard. He'll be so happy. Tell him straight away. We need all the wonderful news there is after the months of worry and fear we've all had. Tell him. There is no taking anything from my day. It has already been far more peculiar than I could ever have imagined. At least this will be a nice surprise."

"Wouldn't it be wonderful if you were to fall pregnant soon as well?" Emily mused. "Our children could grow up as the very best of friends, as we are."

"I'd like to just get married before I think of anything else," Marta said with a grin.

When Father Paul returned with some holy water from the font, Marta splashed some on her face. "This may be the most blessed I have ever been," she said as she wiped her face. Emily and Father Paul grinned.

With a kind smile, the priest ushered them outside through the side door, and made his way back into the church. Marta and Emily linked arms and walked round to the back steps, with excitement bubbling up within them.

Mayor Winston was waiting for them at the main doors. "I was worried where you'd got to," he said, fussing a little at Emily, then at Marta. "I'd find it very hard to give you away if you weren't here."

Emily made a few last adjustments to Marta's dress, then made her way slowly up the aisle of the church, followed by Marta and Mayor Winston. Elias was standing at the front of the church with Father Paul to one side of him and Garrett Harding to the other. Garrett gave Marta a wink as Mayor Winston put her hand into Elias'. When Elias gave her an apologetic look, she smiled warmly at him. What had gone before no longer mattered. This was all about making a new start, for them both.

EPILOGUE

September 12, 1891, Iron Creek, Minnesota

The air was cool, but the sky was a bright blue. Elias whistled to himself as he circled Jet around the herd. The drive to the markets in Duluth had gone well, and he'd managed to purchase Garrett a fine bull and some cows in calf to grow his herd. As he drew closer to Iron Creek, he felt happier than he had ever been. His wife was waiting for him in their cabin, and he would be at home with her throughout the fall and winter. He could hardly wait to see Marta. He had been surprised by just how much he missed her, especially as there had been little opportunity for her to send him any of her wonderful letters as he'd been sleeping out under the stars much of the time.

He waved to his neighbors and friends as he drove the animals along Main Street. Emily and Richard were crossing the street, pushing a large perambulator. Their baby must have been born while he was away. He stopped for a moment and dismounted.

"Congratulations," he said, peering into the perambulator. A chubby-cheeked baby gurgled up at him.

"Yes, a girl. We've named her Alison, for my mother," Richard said happily. "She's a dote. Sleeps well and eats whenever she can."

"She is beautiful, like her mother," Elias said, beaming at Emily.

"Thank you," she said. "I don't feel so beautiful at the moment. Even though she is such a good baby, it's much harder work than you expect."

When he noticed that a couple of the cows had begun to stray, Elias sighed. "I'd best keep them moving," he said. "But I do hope that we will see you both soon?"

"I think Marta planned to have us up for lunch on the first Sunday after you returned, so we shall see you tomorrow," Emily said happily. "I look forward to hearing all about the market and the animals you've bought."

"No, you don't," Elias said with a smile. "Even Garrett will probably be bored when I tell him, but I will tell you of the incredible animals and plants I saw as I drove them home."

"Then I shall look forward to that," she said. "Oh, and before you go, my father and Richard's Aunt Mary have finally announced their engagement. They will be wed in a month's time. I do hope you will be here for that."

"I am not leaving Marta's side until spring," Elias assured her. "I would be delighted to attend. I am glad for them both. They are good for one another, and it will be wonderful for Mayor Winston to have some company in that big house again."

"Yes, he misses Marta a lot."

"And you," Richard pointed out. Suddenly, he laughed. "Elias, you'd best go," he said, pointing to a cow that was munching at the flowers in Mary Jellicoe's window boxes.

With a quick tip of his hat, Elias quickly herded the cows into a group and urged them forward, and then up the mountain.

Garrett beamed as he entered the yard. "You've brought us some fine animals," he said. "But where's the bull?"

"I couldn't bring him with these, but Walter Keeble is coming this way in a month. He said he'd bring him for me. He's a fine beast, big and healthy as they come. Walter's a good cowman, he'll take good care of him in the meantime."

"Well, let's get this lot into the paddock. I thought it best if we keep them there for a few days to rest before they go out with the rest of the herd."

"Definitely for the best," Elias agreed.

Now he was so close to home, Elias found his attention straying to the little cabin just through the thicket, but it didn't take him and Garrett long to get the animals settled.

"Now, get off to your wife," Garrett said with a grin. "She's been missing you."

"I've missed her, too," Elias said.

He urged Jet to a canter and then a gallop. Keeping his head low as they raced through the trees, he felt happier than he had ever been. He had a good job, good friends, and a beautiful wife. He could never have imagined any of that would one day be his. He had everything a man could want, and he was more than grateful for all of it.

Marta was pinning washing out on the line. At the sound of hoofbeats, she looked up and beamed when she saw Elias racing toward her. He dismounted before Jet had even come to a halt, and immediately swept her up in his arms and covered her face with kisses. "I cannot tell you how much I missed you," he said.

"You stink of cow and horse," she said playfully, but she kissed him back, matching his passion for her. "I wasn't expecting you until the middle of the week at least. As glad as I am to have you home, I must finish this or I'll have to do it all again. The sheets will dry musty if they stay in the basket."

"The cows behaved well," he said, reluctantly releasing her from his arms. "I'll fetch the bath in after I've rubbed Jet down. Get rid of the smell?" She nodded and gave him another kiss before continuing to peg out the sheets.

Elias took Jet round to the stall he and Garrett had built for him not long after Elias and Marta had got married, then took off his saddle and bridle and brushed him down before turning him into the stall with some oats and hay.

"Thanks, you've done a fine job, as always," Elias said as he shut the stall door. "I'll be down later with some more hay."

Wearily, he made his way back to the house, grabbing the tin bath as he did so. Inside, a fire was roaring in the grate and Marta had put several big pans full of water on to boil for his bath. He put the bath in front of the fire and stripped off his clothes as she poured the water into the bath. He sank down into the hot water gratefully and smiled when she pulled a stool up beside him and began to soap his back and wash his hair.

"I am so happy you are home," she whispered. "I have the most wonderful news."

"I know, I bumped into Emily and Richard," Elias said. "Mayor Winston and Mrs. Ball are getting married at last. I'm delighted for them both."

Marta chuckled. "No, not that news, though it is indeed wonderful. No, my news is a little more important just for us."

"It is?"

"You're going to be a father," she whispered in his ear. "In the spring."

"You're in calf?" he said, stunned.

"How dare you!" she protested with a giggle. "We're going to have a baby, not another cow for you to look after."

Elias stared at her, then pulled her to him, not caring one bit that he was still in the bath. She squealed as she hit the water, but he soon silenced her with a long, lingering kiss.

"I thought I was the happiest man alive, just having you. But you've just made it even better. Thank you for giving this weary cowboy a second chance, I don't think I will ever deserve all the joy you have brought into my life, but I am grateful for every bit of it."

"You changed your life, not me." She replied. "You were already this man, long before I met you. And you're still on your first chance with me. It was you that gave yourself a second chance. I love you, Elias Groves."

"I love you more, Marta Groves," he murmured softly, full of joy in the knowledge that this cowboy had indeed been blessed with a second chance and much, much more.

The End

OTHER SERIES BY KARLA

Sun River Brides

Ruby Springs Brides

Silver River Brides

Eagle Creek Brides

Iron Creek Brides

Faith Creek Brides

CONNECT WITH KARLA GRACEY

Visit my website at www.karlagracey.com to sign up to my newsletter and get free books and be notified as to when my new releases are available.

Printed in Great Britain
by Amazon